The Emperor of Nuts

ELAINE BARNARD

The Emperor of Nuts

intersections across cultures

LIBRARY OF CONGRESS CATALOGING-IN-PUBLICATION DATA
The Emperor of Nuts
Authored by Elaine Barnard
ISBN: 9780999461747
LCCN: 2018945748

contents

Emperor of Nuts

YOU WILL FIND ME in my kitchen every morning during the rainy season. Wind howls through the patio. Rain washes the clothes hung out to dry. My kittens yowl in their cages outside waiting for breakfast, for freedom from the night's predators, feral cats and wild dogs roaming the alleys or other beasts descending from the hillsides surrounding us. Soon I will tend to them, allow them to play in the house, to sleep on the sofa despite my wife's reservations. "The sun will be out today," I say to quiet them. But they do not believe me. Somehow, they know it is a lie.

I buy my peanuts from the kampung market where they are cheap. In the city center of Ipoh, there are a few small shops where you can bargain for shelled or unshelled. I always buy shelled. It would be less expensive to buy unshelled, but then I would have to crack them. At one time I would ask my daughters to do this. But they no longer live here. That is, they do, and they don't. One is at school in Europe. Another lives with her fiancé while we pretend she lives at home should the nosy neighbors inquire. A third lives here when it's convenient and with her friends when it's not.

All three are planning to marry in the dry season when the sun scorches Malaysia, and the sky is sultry with smog. The heat leaves you limp and perspiring, while the bill for air conditioning climbs. That is my worry. That is why I am making the peanut butter. I will give it as gifts to their hundreds of friends and relatives. That way I will build up a clientele who will surely love my product and order more. Gradually I will raise the price year by year, hardly noticeable. Eventually, I will hire some maciks from the kampung to help me. I will advertise. I will capture the market. Thus, I hope to repay the loans that will afford their nuptials.

I take my old food processor from the shelf and grind the nuts praying the blades do not jam as they did yesterday. I love the smell of fresh peanuts, pungent but sweet. For a moment I exist on a tidal wave of nuts. The whole room whirls like the blender. I add a pinch of salt to enhance the nutty flavor. I never add sugar or oil like Jiffy does or Skippy or other imported butters. No, my butter is pure, free from all preservatives, all additives. It is natural. I will include this on the labels.

My wife bought the jars yesterday on her way home from the architectural firm where she is lucky enough to still have a job. She has been passed over many times for promotions. It could be her age, or her gender, who can say? Of course, I never mention such things as they would upset her. Then she would not speak to me for weeks, even though we share a bed and bathroom.

I pour the butter into the jars. They glisten beneath the lamplight, brown jewels worth much more than my asking price. Now you are probably wondering why I must sell peanut butter when my wife has a job? Have you ever afforded three weddings in one season, paid for the bridal gowns, the hotels, the musicians, banquets, limousines, and so on?

Of course, I have always wished for my daughters to marry, but not all at once. That is why I have gotten many small jobs since my retirement from the engineering firm where I computed the cost of our designs day in and day out. I hated that work. It did nothing for my soul if such a thing exists. I am not a religious person, but still, I feel there is something out there, a hint of something beyond us. I think that might be why I have also been gaining weight. Eating peanut butter each day gives me comfort. It is filling and stays with you for hours like an old friend.

"Retire," I say to her when she returns with the jars, tired from dodging the traffic.

"Retire?" she grumbles. "Can the Emperor of Nuts pay for the weddings? Can he buy the feasts, the hotels for the friends we've never met and the relatives so distant we can't remember their names?"

Of course, she is right. My salary supported their education, all three of them in foreign universities where a degree guaranteed a good position in Malaysia.

I myself was a graduate of the University of Washington. That's how I got the job I hated.

The jars are full now, but I am empty. The house is silent. I wish for the laughter of my daughters when they were little, for their muddy footprints on the floor, their arms around my neck, the perfume of their freshly washed hair. I paste the labels on the jars, "EMPEROR OF NUTS" and line them on my kitchen counter in gleaming rows. The glass reflects the promise of sunshine. But the rain keeps falling.

Great Satan
Meets the Axis of Evil

IT'S SLOW SEASON in Tehran, cold and rainy, freezing my bones even though I'm dressed in a thick blue *roopoosh* that covers my butt, and my favorite pink *roosari* crocheted by my mother in the hope that the hot pink head scarf would attract a future husband. So much for that.

Most tourists go to some tropical paradise. I'd rather be in some bikini clime as well. But my job is to guide Great Satan around Tehran. I'm a government guide, one of the few authorized to guide Americans, the only woman, and at twenty-seven, the youngest. I take pride in my knowledge of our former glory. Ask me anything about our World Heritage sites, and I will answer truthfully not like some other guides who fabricate answers to entertain the tourists. But if you ask me political questions I will only smile feigning ignorance.

Great Satan is here on the cheap. My tour costs double in high season, April or May. The flowers bloom in Tehran then. It is pleasantly warm, not burning hot like July and August when I long to tear the scarf off my head but dare not for fear of the religious police.

I call Etihad Air to make certain Great Satan's plane has arrived, and my Americans are waiting at the Parasto Hotel. The Parasto is a two-star in the electronics section of Tehran. Every other store here sells either LG or Samsung. Their room is small and dark facing a concrete wall. The showerhead is handheld, but the toilet is Western which pleases most Americans who hate squatting over an Eastern hole.

I'm supposed to pick them up at 9 a.m. Some of my hair is peeking from my scarf which I think is rather sexy. My hair is sort of auburn. My parents tell me it's beautiful. I'm waiting for some guy to tell me that too. Not that I want to get married. I prefer being independent, having a career, my own money. But I must admit I love babies. If I could have a baby without being married, it would be divine. But then I would be a disgrace to my family. My father sent me to a private university at great expense to become a geneticist, not a tour guide. However, I enjoy talking to people. Being imprisoned in a lab all day would suffocate me. This is a great disappointment to my mother and father.

When I arrive at the Parasto, my Americans are eating breakfast. It's not a bad breakfast but not good either, boiled eggs rather than omelets, cheap *sangat* (one of my country's many flatbreads), olives, cucumbers, feta cheese, and dates. I pop into the dining room for some *halwah* (I've always had a sweet tooth) before

I greet my clients. It's difficult to tour Americans. They have no embassy here to help them should they get into trouble. I'd been hoping for some handsome Italians, but then I'd have to spend the whole morning finding espresso for them. "Hotel coffee is shitty," they say. "Why don't you smoke, Nadia? It's relaxing." I tried it once to please my Italians by lighting up in the midst of Tehran's wild traffic. I nearly choked to death.

I observe my clients before I greet them. The man is rather attractive in a Western way, pale and blue-eyed, but older than my father. Nevertheless, I apply more rose lipstick to look my best, thinking he might have a young friend back in America that I could Skype with. His mother is small and quiet. She keeps her eyes down like a modest Iranian matron would.

I'm hoping the Parasto has a room for me this time, instead of a closet. We'll be in Tehran two days before we fly to Shiraz. I could sleep at home, but that has become difficult since my twin sisters were born. My parents have a two-bedroom apartment in a decent part of Tehran, but I have four siblings there. Mother and Father occupy one bedroom with the twins, and my two younger sisters live in the other. There is no longer a place for me. I'm homeless, so I stay in hotels when I guide and with friends when I don't. At one time my family had a big apartment. My sisters and I went to private schools with swimming, calligraphy, English and French lessons. When the Sanctions started, however, my dad lost his job in the oil fields, and all that was over. Now he sits at home hoping the economy will improve, Sanctions will be lifted, and he might find work again. I try to help out when I can when the tourist season is booming. But currently, it's all I can do to feed myself. Recently I toured two French guys, really hot. My ship had come in. But just as soon it went out. They were gay.

"Good morning, did you sleep well?" I always say this knowing they probably didn't. The Parasto's beds are not famous for comfort.

"So-so." Mother answers. Deep circles under her watery eyes.

"Not bad," her son perks up." When you're tired, you sleep."

"You snore," the old lady grumbles.

"So do you," the son jokes offering me some coffee.

"No thanks, I'm wired for the day. I'll go over the top with coffee."

This isn't true. I long for a cup of coffee, but in Iran, it is not polite to accept the first time something's offered. It is Iranian *taarof* to wait until something is offered three times before you accept. But he doesn't offer again. The American way.

"Are you ready for an amazing day? The National Museum is first on our list."

"Nadia," the old lady reads my name tag, "I'd like to brush my teeth before we start out."

What is this teeth brushing obsession? Did she make a twenty-hour plane flight at great expense just to brush her teeth? She should forget her teeth, live in anticipation of the wonders that await her.

"Of course," I smile, snagging another chunk of *halwah*. "Take your time."

She trots up the stairs to their room. We wait and wait for her to return.

"Do you think she's all right?"

"Oh yes, Mother's always like this. She brushes after every meal. Even a snack disturbs her until she's brushed. Her first husband was a dentist. 'Decay occurs immediately after eating,' he always said. "She divorced him but never forgot his mantra."

The old lady clops down the stairs in heavy boots, a trench coat, and a black *roosari*. "I'm ready now," she smiles showing off her freshly brushed teeth.

We walk out into the rain. They forgot to bring umbrellas, so we squeeze under mine, the old lady taking up most of the room with her five layers of clothing. The streets are slick with garbage. Wind collapses my umbrella.

The smell of roasting kabobs from street vendors reminds me that I'm still hungry. But a real sit-down breakfast is something I haven't had in years. Mostly because I prefer to sleep until the last minute, then pick up a bite on the fly. There's something energizing about this as if a full meal might cause inertia.

It's about a thirty-minute walk from the Parasto to Tehran's National Museum, a monolithic structure established in 1937. I love the arched entrance and always pause before going in so my clients can admire the beauty of the brick walls, the swerve of the ceiling designed by the French architect Andre Godard in the early twentieth century. The old lady is having some trouble climbing the steps, so we brace her elbows and whisk her up. Inside are three main halls full of archeology which I do my best to explain knowing it is too much information in a single morning. So, I leave them on their own but not before I point out my favorite exhibit, the Salt Man from Zajan, a miner who died in the third or fourth century AD but whose white-bearded head, leg in a leather boot and tools were preserved by the salt in which he was buried. The old lady seems entranced by him, so I disappear into the cafe across the courtyard for a cup of coffee with my friend, Hamid, who manages the cafe. Hamid is always telling me he'll have to close shop soon if the Sanctions aren't lifted. "The inflation is killing me." He wipes down a table with a dirty rag. "I can afford nothing."

It's still raining when we rush through Tehran's pollution to my favorite restaurant for lunch. I should have worn my special Nox face mask, the one with the filters. I feel a cough coming on, but I don't want to frighten my clients. The restaurant is crowded with Australians who can travel here and get their visa on arrival without the elaborate steps required of Americans. It's only the Americans, Canadians, and Brits, the three without embassies who are restricted, who need a government guide or they could be arrested. We sit next to an Australian wedding party. I find it difficult to understand the Aussies, so I let my Americans do all the talking.

I order lamb stew sweetened with pomegranate and rice. We always have rice, sometimes three different kinds. Rice keeps us strong. While we wait they bring us an appetizer of olives, pickles, cucumbers, tomatoes, and feta. I love food, all its textures and flavors. I feel I could live just for food. I dream of opening my own B&B in the style of the old houses of Tehran with a spacious courtyard filled with flowers and low tables with soft cushions for eating and comfortable rooms surrounding the courtyard for sleeping. The courtyard would be canopied so my guests would be protected from the rain. I would serve ample meals with many courses, and great feasts on holidays such as our Naruz, the Iranian New Year that celebrates the Spring Equinox. Tourists would come from everywhere to visit my inn. I'll call it The Caspian, like the sea, ever changing, but always beautiful.

When I finally tear them away from the Australians, we head for the Grand Bazaar. "Wait until we get to Shiraz to shop. The stuff is real there. In Tehran, everything is cheap because everything is made in China."

The old lady drops a large Prada purse. She'd been examining the price tag. "It's hard to resist a bargain," she grumbles.

I pick them up early the next morning for our 8 a.m. flight to Shiraz. They were too early for breakfast at the

Parasto so I promise the food on Iran Air will prevent starvation. We squeeze into the battered taxi. I chat with the driver in Farsi to keep myself awake. (I was out last night circling the malls with my good friend Nilofer. All the boys asked for her number. No one asked for mine. (I think maybe I'm getting a bit flabby from all that Nutella over ice cream at midnight.)

Sometimes Nilofer and I go to the cinema. I often go alone. I adore romantic movies in Farsi or old American films with Audrey Hepburn. "Breakfast at Tiffany's" is my favorite. I wish I were thinner and had black hair like Nilofer or Audrey. Nilofer will soon be married I'm sure, and I will be left to babysit her kids in my off-season.

The old lady complains about the food on Iran Air. A cheese sandwich doesn't cut it. "I was hoping for bacon and eggs," she whines.

"Mom, Muslims don't eat pork, remember?"

"I bet I'd get bacon and eggs on British Air." She spoons yogurt into her parched lips.

"Yogurt's better for you, Mom." He pats her hand. "Remember what the doctor said."

"I'm on vacation. I should have what I want." She slams down the spoon.

"Look this way, Mom, and smile." He snaps her photo on his phone. She forgets about the bacon.

When we land in Shiraz, I hire a taxi to drive us to Persepolis.

"We could be in California," the old lady says wiping some grime off the window. We pass the arid

Zagros Mountains, a high desert landscape dotted with piles of cinder block homes and offices reinforced with steel for earthquakes, some coated with aluminum paint to reflect the brutal summer sun.

The old lady is nodding off when several hours later we finally reach the plains of Persepolis. "I could use a cup of coffee," she yawns as if we're about to see a movie instead of one of the world's greatest architectural sites.

"Coffee it is, Mom."

Her son is so agreeable. (Mom probably paid for the trip.)

Reinforced with coffee and cookies, we climb the stairs to the first platform of Persepolis only to see another higher platform which holds the Apadana Palace. This is the place where the king held his receptions.

The Gate of All Nations, also known as the Gate of Xerses is one of the first things we see. This gate bears inscriptions in three languages. "Be kind to travelers and respect other people's cultures."

He takes photos of his mother beside the beheaded limestone columns. Alexander the Great did a super job trashing this palace. Apparently, he ignored the maxims on the gate.

I amble off to the cafe to chat in Farsi with Reza, the owner. It's such an effort to speak English all day. When I used to guide the French, they corrected my mistakes, but the Americans never do. I wish they would so I could improve.

When an hour later I climb back up to find them, they wave from the highest platform. The old lady actually smiles. Then I discover she is just posing for another photo op.

Our hotel, the Karim Khan, is luxurious compared to the Parasto. Same price, but Tehran is very crowded, so everything costs more than in surrounding cities. "Sleep well," I tell them. "Tomorrow we bus to Isfahan."

"I'd like to take a run before we leave," the son says carting their luggage upstairs.

"Make sure you carry some I.D." Not that it would do him any good should the police pick him up for wandering the streets without me.

I was relieved to see him all packed in the morning. "Great run," he grins sweat brimming his brow.

"You still have time for a shower," I advise, knowing the bus would be crowded. A sweaty American would not be welcome.

"Mom's in the shower. She takes a long time. I'll air dry before we board."

When the old lady finally appears, I seat us near the back of the bus so her son can air dry. She reclines her chair and immediately starts snoring while her son starts snapping more photos. He's always so busy taking photos that I think maybe he really doesn't see anything. The camera's focus is limited. I don't own a camera for fear I might miss the whole scene.

Isfahan was once the capital of ancient Persia, larger than London and more cosmopolitan than Paris. Now it's home to one of Iran's nuclear conversion facilities that were the cause of the Sanctions. I don't mention this to my clients. Instead, I take them to the Naqsh-e Jahan Square and Ali Qas, where Shah Abbas watched polo players from his balcony. Today the square sparkles with fountains. The winter sun warms the tourists. We watch the craftsmen hammering copper into elegant blue plates.

"I'll buy one." The old lady points to a huge copper dish.

"You can't fit it into your suitcase, Mom. Buy a smaller one."

"I want that one."

"We can ship." The craftsman smiles.

She changes her mind when he tells her the price for shipping. "I think I'll just take that smaller one. I can fit it into my purse."

That night we spend at the Safir Hotel. The old lady loves it. They have an elevator.

In the morning we visit the Armenian Vank cathedral. The priest shows us around. "Not many visitors anymore. I say mass for no one. It seems the whole world is secular."

When did I last go to the mosque or say my prayers? My grandparents say prayers five times a day. My parents attend the mosque on holy days if my dad is home. (Mother still doesn't drive.) Religion is for old people, like ancient history. It's never done anything but get us into wars from Alexander the Great until now.

The next afternoon we drive back to Tehran. I avoid showing them the American Embassy graffiti on all the walls, "Death to America," "Go Home Satan," and much worse. Instead, I take them to the Contemporary Art Museum which holds both Iran's modern masters and hundreds of works by some of the giants of Western modernism—Warhol, Giacometti, Oldenburg—not seen outside Iran since they were collected by the Shah's wife, Farah, in the 1970s. We protect these works, a cultural legacy worth millions. If the economy defaults, we can sell the art.

Tonight, we say farewell in a little cafe near the Parasto. Our waiter is decorated with tattoos, which amaze the old lady, since she heard they were forbidden in Islam. (We imitate the West despite our isolation.)

We kiss each other three times on the cheek, as is Iranian custom. The old lady has tears in her eyes. I think I might have some in mine as well. Her son presses some money into my hand. "I'm about to refuse, Iranian style, but then I recall the American custom. Better to say yes at once. To hell with etiquette. The tip is warm in my fingers. I remember my parents, their hopeless expression on my last visit. This will keep the wolf from their door. At least for a while.

Bridge of No Return

EACH MORNING before I open my shop to the tourists I cross the Bridge of No Return and attach another prayer ribbon to the fence. There are thousands of ribbons there now, thousands praying for the reunification of Korea.

I shiver in the frigid December chill, bundled in my heavy boots and parka, for a last glimpse across the bridge, hoping to see my father somewhere on the horizon. I know this is foolish as he was taken by the Communists so many years ago. My mother says the Communists must have dragged my father across the bridge when, on night patrol, he mistakenly came too near their outposts. He could be dead by now or if not dead, so elderly that it would be impossible for him to escape. I inhale the fragrance of the river below as I wait, the foliage that flourishes on its banks undisturbed by the guns and soldiers guarding it. It is a dream that I have, that one day he will appear, the father I lost when I was just a tiny girl.

Buses arrive daily delivering curious visitors from every part of the globe to the Demilitarized Zone in

Seoul. They crowd my shop buying DMZ T-shirts, caps, nail clippers, back packs, and even wine from the North. Wine is about all you can buy from the North now as the South has put a ban on trade as long as the North continues its testing of nukes. The tourists are very excited as they clamber from the buses. They shout and giggle across the parking lot. It's a day's outing for them, a fun filled morning exploring the tunnels dug after the war by the North Koreans in a plan to eventually invade Seoul. One defector told me the North dug as many as twenty tunnels. The youth love to pretend they are soldiers sneaking into enemy territory. I have been in the Third Tunnel myself. It is dark and dank. Water drips from its narrow walls.

The roof would have bumped my head if I hadn't crouched on my way to the exit. I could hardly breathe as I climbed out even though ventilation had been installed. But in the early days there was no ventilation for the 30,000 troops with which the North had planned to invade the South. If your lungs were not strong you probably died in there gasping for the slightest hint of air.

It is time to open my shop now. I turn back into the turbid morning. A sprinkle of rain descends from the wayward clouds, promising a deluge later. A strange sadness overcomes me as I open my doors to the visitors rushing from the myriad of buses polluting the air. I try not to inhale the toxins. The youth are properly attired, no ripped jeans, T-shirts, flip flops, shorts or miniskirts.

The DMZ authorities are strict. Some say it is a matter of respect for the gravity of the occasion. Others say the North would take pictures of those shabbily dressed and use it as propaganda depicting the poverty of the South rather than admitting it is just a fashion trend.

My shop was formerly managed by my mother. But she is in her eightieth year now, and the frailties of age are upon her. We share a one room apartment in the less prosperous part of Seoul. There aren't many pensions here, nor much old age insurance, so to supplement my small income, my mother collects cardboard and old papers, piles them in her cart and sells them to companies who recycle the lot into goods for the tourists. Nothing goes to waste here except lives. We are an ecologically minded economy.

When I have a day off, I take my mother for a stroll on the bridge. She totters along looking wistfully across the river, hoping as I do that Father will somehow appear. Her gnarled fingers caress the prayer ribbons as she reads them. Carefully, she attaches one more, a yellow ribbon, her prayer for his return printed upon it.

"It is getting late. We should go home now," I murmur as her eyes fill with tears. I do not want her to cry. It is too painful for me and devastating for her. Her body trembles. I have to hold her.

"Mother, little Mother, "I whisper as rain dampens the ribbons fluttering in the frigid wind sweeping up from the river. "Look, I see his shadow. He is waiting for us on the other side."

House of Mirrors

"WAIT FOR ME," he'd said, "down here beneath our house. I have dug a cave for you. It will be safe. By the time your provisions are gone, I will be back."

The desert winds blew hard and dry filling my cave with their acrid odor. Breathing became a daily chore. Still, I waited, but Khalifa did not return. It was then I started smashing things, mostly mirrors that had been discarded as Kuwait fled the Iraqi invasion. Why would a refugee need a mirror? What an absurdity to haul a mirror when you could hardly haul yourself, your wife and children.

The mirrors were everywhere, so I began collecting them. It gave me great pleasure to watch them crack, blow by blow, like the hearts of those to whom they once belonged now on the perilous journey to nowhere.

I will make a house of mirrors, I thought, to light their way home, to light his way home, Khalifa, my husband of many years, gone without a sound, as if some ghost had captured him. Yes, the reflection would tell him I was waiting, that I was here to salve his wounds.

It was then I heard it, a kind of moaning or weeping outside my door. I was afraid to open it for fear it was some animal that might leap inside, circle the house in a rage if I didn't feed it. But the moans gradually subsided into a kind of keening. Now, I thought, such a creature could hardly be dangerous. Pressing myself against the door, I opened it slowly, just a crack at first. And there, staring at herself in the mirrored doorway was a creature neither young nor old. Her face had been so badly burned it was difficult to tell her age. But I knew she was female because her abdomen protruded from her ragged covering as if the fetus was struggling to survive regardless of the chaos beyond.

The woman was so exhausted she could hardly stand, so I scooped her into my arms and lay her on the mirrored couch which I had just completed. I tried to place a pillow beneath her head, but she refused. It seemed the hard glass suited her. I offered some rainwater with a squeeze of old lemon from the garden. She sipped like a cat licking the drops into her mouth. Then she fell asleep.

In the morning I tried to wake her but I could not. Her mouth lay open as if she were trying to call someone for help, perhaps a loved one, perhaps me.

I wet some towels and trickled the drops on her ravaged face, slowly, carefully so the liquid would soothe her. Gradually, she opened her eyes regarding me as if she wasn't sure where she was or even who.

I continued to bathe her thinking eventually the water would bring her mind back. "They took me," she squeezed the words from her lips as if each syllable was a kind of agony.

"Who took you?"

"They took me…" she repeated again and again until the words became a chant. Then she started to weep in that strange animal sound that I'd heard outside my door.

"Sleep," I said, "sleep." A vague smile distorted her burned lips. I shuddered to think of what she must have endured. I went to the cabinet and found some expired antibiotics that I had hidden when the Iraqis stormed Kuwait City. Stripping some old sheets into bandages, I spread a layer of medication on the cloth and pressed it to her face. She did not scream as I feared she might but succumbed to the treatment like an animal grateful to have its wounds healed.

"Did you see him?" I whispered against her blood-soaked ear. "Was there any sign of my husband?"

"Your husband?" she replied in a daze.

"Khalifa… Khalifa, the artist?"

"There-there is no-no such person."

"There must be."

"If-if there is, he-he no longer answers to his name…"

Then she began to howl like a dog. It almost seemed as if she'd become part animal. I petted her crusted hair, her slumped shoulders, her scabbed arms and legs. It seemed to comfort her.

In the days that followed she would not walk but crawled through the rubble that had become my home.

She lay at the foot of my bed at night, gently snoring her animal snore. We were as comfortable on the mirrored slabs as if they were filled with down. I fed her bowls of milk from the black market that had sprung up in Kuwait's inner depths. She followed me everywhere. However, I had to put a leash on her to keep her out of trouble. She had a habit of growling at dogs and hissing at cats if they came near me. I was afraid they might hurt her as she was still recovering from her wounds. Also, the child, if that's what it was, grew larger by the month and would soon be too heavy for her to carry along the ground without injuring it. I worried as well that she might cut herself on the shards of glass that flew everywhere as I worked. But she somehow avoided them. Instead, she gathered the shards into sparkling piles so that I could glue the small pieces into designs on the glass chairs, couch and love seat that I was constructing in the hope of Khalifa's return. I had been an architect in our early life together, but this new-found skill would surely astonish him.

We worked day and night as if in a trance. The outside world had little meaning for us. It was the mirrors we wanted, the glass house that could not be destroyed because we would rebuild it.

Shadows

"*NOVEMBER IS A GOOD TIME* to be in Kuwait. It's cooler now, not like summer. It can reach 130 degrees then." Rasheed wiped his brow with the back of his hand and squinted at the lights burning in the airport's vast interior.

I did not reply. The Philippines were also hot in summer. I was used to sweating.

"This household where I am taking you for the work, Asria, is air-conditioned, a mansion. You'll see how beautiful."

I smiled when he winked at me not looking down at my feet as my sister had taught. No, this time I met his eyes to see if there was truth in them. But I could not tell. There was a haze behind his glasses that kept me from seeing truly.

My number was finally called. "Go—go." Rasheed pushed me toward Immigration. The officer took a long time examining my passport as if he was certain he'd find something amiss. But I knew it was in order. Rasheed had made sure it was so.

I stood at attention, my feet straight ahead, arms at my sides so the officer could find no fault. My dress was also modest. I wore a light sweater over it. "The night air can be chilly. Wear something warm," Rasheed had advised.

However, I did not have anything really warm. I never needed it in Manila. This light sweater, borrowed from my older sister was all I had.

Just as my knees started to shake, the officer stamped my passport and issued my visa. Rasheed took me by the elbow, "Good girl." He jostled me through the hordes of anxious immigrants to the exit.

I dragged my small suitcase. Rasheed took it from me. "You must be tired. That was a long trip."

Yes, I was exhausted. I had been up since early yesterday preparing to come, not wanting to leave home really but what home did I have? My sister and I rented a room in the poorest section of Manila. We spent our days scavenging the garbage dumps behind KFC for chicken parts. My sister would recook the pieces in palm oil with bits of wilted vegetables. I tried selling our product on street corners but began vomiting from the smell before I'd sold a single portion. "This is not for you," she said. "You have to toughen up."

I thought I had a better chance in life by leaving the country of my birth. "Filipinas needed," the advertisement read. "Work in Kuwait for stable and reliable families." Why not? I would have a family that cared. It was so long since anyone had. Even my sister had grown tired of me.

Outside the airport the night was brisk. I buttoned my sweater. "You should have brought something warmer." Rasheed slipped into his faded leather jacket. He was not much older than me, still in his late teens or early twenties, scrawny and tall with the scars of acne. I could never love him. There was something about him; something in the way he shuffled his feet that bothered me, something in the stoop of his shoulders...

"Wait here," he said. "I'll get the car."

The dusky night closed around me. A wind blew in from the Gulf sweeping sand into my eyes, my throat, leaving a fine layer of dust on my suitcase. I longed for the moist air of Manila.

A whistle from across the street. Rasheed stood beside his vehicle beckoning me to cross. But how could I in all this traffic? I stood frozen as the lampposts surrounding me while men in passing autos honked, opening their doors. "Come," they hooted, "Come."

Finally, Rasheed came. Grabbing me, he shoved me into the traffic. "What's wrong with you, girl?" We rushed between braking cars. "You need some guts in this city. They don't wait for you, so you don't wait for them."

His automobile was sleek, like an old hearse that had been refurbished. "You can sit up front with me. Take a nap. It'll be a long while before we get there. Your family lives on the other side of town, the better side." He patted my knee.

I could not close my eyes. The lights on the freeway bled into them. Huge skyscrapers loomed beneath a fierce moon. "We're passing the Grand Mosque, Asria. Look quickly. Once you start working, you might not see it again."

"Why not?" I murmured sleepily, dazed by the floodlights bathing the Mosque's dome.

"You will soon see," he laughed and gunned the motor.

I fell forward. He thrust his arm across my chest. "Sorry," he smiled. "Better tighten that seat belt."

We drove past McDonald's, past the Friday Market. The Market was still open even at this late hour. Women with babies wandered about in their black abayas examining rugs, clothing, and cutlery through the slits in their niqabs. How could they see? How could they balance? As we slowed for a light, children tossed soda cans and candy wrappers from car windows. My thirst increased. How I would love to have a sip of that soda before it hit the ground.

"We're almost there," Rasheed said as we left the piles of debris choking the city's center. The rancid odor of rotting vegetables and fruit followed us. Soon we drove through long streets lined with high walls protecting concrete mansions. We stopped in front of a wall topped with broken glass. A night watchman hovered behind the gate adjusting his tattered turban. "Asalalmu alaykum," peace be upon you, Rasheed greeted him.

"Mualaykum salam," and also with you, the old watchman returned.

Rasheed pushed me inside and slung my suitcase after me. "If things don't work out," he shouted, "call me. I'll drive you to the airport." He honked his horn and was gone.

The watchman rubbed sand from his eyes, ran gnarly fingers through his beard and led me in silence up the sandy drive toward the white mansion glittering in the moonlight. "You sweep drive tomorrow early." He kicked aside a sand drift that had blown in from the surrounding desert. "Must be clean before Sir drives off. Sand in his tire he does not like."

I shook my head as if I understood but really did not. The sand would always blow in. Where would I dispose of it before more sand engulfed us? But I would not ask such a question.

Such a question might send me packing back to Manila.

He unlocked the huge wooden door and led me down a marble hallway. I glimpsed the living room. It was lined with silken couches beside golden lamps. Gilded porcelain urns loomed in the corners bursting with artificial flowers. High ceiling spotlights lit the room. If I could only lie down on one of those couches, I would be happy.

Eventually, we arrived at the kitchen. It gleamed with every appliance I'd seen in the magazines at the airport. "You sleep here." He parted a beaded curtain. Behind it lay a small cot big enough for a child. A uniform of yellow pajamas, blouse, and apron hung on the wall. "In back toilet and tub. Clean mops there."

The curtain shuddered as he shuffled back through the kitchen and down the hallway to his post outside. The heavy door groaned as he left.

I fell onto the cot hugging my knees; then I rocked myself to sleep as I had when I was little.

———

In the dim morning light, the watchman hovered over me. "Rise child. Family chores."

"When will I meet this family?"

"To meet you they do not care. Soon you see."

"But—"

"Sh…" he cautioned. "You be shadow person like me. It is best."

I had foolishly hoped that it would be different, that perhaps my family would grow to love me. Maybe they will yet, I thought.

"Dress quick. Soon Sir will be up. He can no be late for hospital. Patients wait. Some travel from far to see him."

Quickly I dressed and went to the kitchen. I splashed water on my face and was about to dry it with a rag when in the mirror above the sink I saw a beautiful image. A girl, about my own age, eighteen years or so, stood at the entrance to the kitchen. "My espresso," she clicked her ruby fingernails. "I expect it as soon as I wake."

"Sorry. No one told me…" I lowered my eyes and turned toward the shadows as the watchman had advised.

———

"Well, I'm telling you now. At this time every morning I expect coffee in my bedroom, also some Naan. Perhaps a few dates too or figs, whatever's in season in our garden." She tossed her ebony hair. It fell across her robe like a silken shawl. Her lips pouted and her glistening eyes, still full of sleep, slowly turned from me as if she hardly saw me, as if I were simply a bit of dust or a mop waiting to clean the floor. I heard her stomp back up the marble staircase. She slammed the door to her bedroom. I hurried into the garden to examine the trees for fresh figs. The date palms were so tall I knew I could never harvest them without some help. The old watchman might know—

"Child," he was behind me. "The sand—You have not swept. Sir will be angry."

"The girl came and—"

"Ah, that Fauzia. She bad tempered until her coffee come. Did you bring?"

"I did not know I should. No one—"

"You must know without us say."

"I—I…"

"You come to Om for help. I know little but do my best. Here figs." Expertly he pulled some from the branches without bruising them. "Wash them careful. Place in silver bowl with a bit of cream and sugar. Serve each morning unless the dates be ripe. She prefer the dates. She like to lick stones when through."

"But the sand?"

"I sweep for you this morning. Tomorrow rise earlier so you sweep before prepare coffee. Now that her mother has passed, Fauzia mistress here."

"Please help me with the machine. There are so many."

"Soon you master coffee machine. For now, press this switch only. Four cups in silver pot from Iran is what she want. But now I hurry. Sir rise soon."

"Should I—"

"He take breakfast at the hospital."

"Om?" a voice from the driveway.

"I displease him." Grabbing a broom, he scuttled out swinging it before him.

"Hurry Om." It was Sir's voice in the drive, mellow, soft curves around his syllables, so different from Fauzia's sharp edges.

"I'm already late," he said. "Didn't you tell that new Filipina to clean my drive first thing in the morning?"

"Yes Sir, but she arrived late and did not know."

"Well see to it that she knows or I will have to replace her. Things are not the same here since my wife passed." I heard him pause for a moment in prayer. "Make sure Fauzia comes down today. It is not good for her to stay in her room mourning her mother. Her wedding day must be prepared for."

I watched from the shadows as his car ground down the drift strewn drive. Then I rushed about the kitchen spilling coffee and olive oil, wiping up and spilling again before I assembled Fauzia's breakfast neatly on a tray. I started up the stairs to her room trying not to slip as Om had recently mopped them. She did not answer my knock, so I set the tray outside her door.

"Go away," she called. "I'm no longer hungry. I shall stay in bed all day."

"But your father—"

"My father doesn't have to know. Make sure you don't tell him."

My stomach lurched. I had no intention of telling her father. But what if he asked?

Don't think about it I told myself. Just busy yourself with what needs to be done. But where should I start? I went outside where Om was sweeping. "Om," I pleaded as the hours yawned before me, "where do I begin?"

"Begin at beginning." He turned back to his sweeping.

I retreated to the kitchen and filled a bucket with soapy water to mop the floor.

"What are you doing?" Suddenly Fauzia was behind me.

"I thought—"

"It is not your place to think. It is your place to see that the kitchen is clean. You can begin on your knees." She handed me a scrub brush and some rags. "This is how you will wash the kitchen floor and all the other floors as well." She tightened the red sash around her slender waist and left the room trailing a faint essence of rose perfume.

I scrubbed well into the late afternoon, my knees burning, my hands raw from the harsh soap and scalding water. There was no time for breakfast or lunch as whenever I paused Fauzia would somehow appear from nowhere with new orders for me. Om slipped me a crust of bread or some figs whenever he could. But still I was hungry. I had thought my hunger in Manila was bad. However, I'd never known anything like this constant gnawing in my belly.

That night I collapsed on my bed grateful to lie down at last. But in the middle of my sleep I heard something stir. My eyes searched the darkness. There behind the beaded curtain was a figure. I held my breath not daring to speak wondering how long it had stood there. It drew back the curtain slightly. A breeze ruffled the beads. Then, just as I was about to scream, it disappeared.

In the morning I rose at dawn and rushed to the drive to sweep before Sir appeared. When he came, he gave me a sidelong glance, stamped sand from his feet and swung his lean body into the gleaming Porsche. From the shadows I watched him adjust the white gutra on his thick wavy hair. The crisp shoulders of his dishdasha were erect behind the wheel. The roar of his motor thrilled me.

"She come soon." Om was beside me. "Hurry, make coffee before she scold."

I ran into the kitchen. Fauzia stood beside the espresso machine challenging me to begin. She clenched a broom as if she would strike me. I tried to hide, to withdraw into the shadows, but as I parted the beaded curtain of my room, I felt a blow on my back.

I tried to crawl beneath my cot, but there was no need. Without a word, she was gone. I grasped the edge of the cot to help me rise, feeling a burning sensation where she had struck me.

Om waited at the kitchen door leading to the garden. He pressed some figs into my apron pocket. "Her blows do not remember. I have many. I forget."

I nibbled a fig for energy hoping my strength would return. Then I assembled her coffee and bread and climbed the slippery stairs to her room hoping she was asleep, that I could leave her breakfast at the door. But she answered my knock. "Come in," she said sweetly as if this was a different person than the one who struck me. Her bed was hidden by filmy veils. She rested behind them. "I am to be married soon. It is my father's wish."

A satin bridal gown was draped across the couch. Wall mirrors everywhere reflected its elegance. "Stay where you are. Do not come near me."

The veils trembled as she turned away. "You may leave my breakfast on the side table. It is so kind of you to bring it. Leave quietly. Pretend you were never here."

As I withdrew the door swung sharply catching my hand, squeezing it until I cried out. Then she was beside me releasing it. "Asria," she whispered, "even the doors do not know you."

It was dark when I finished my chores each day. The mansion remained silent as if no one lived there. Om usually dozed at his post outside. Even the palms were quiet. No breeze stirred inside the thick walls. I longed for a breeze, some sign of life as I crawled into my cot hoping to get some sleep. Deep sleep had disappeared from my life. I only dozed during the brief hours of rest afraid I would not wake in time to sweep the drive or brew the coffee. Also, I was alert for signs as that same figure appeared each night behind the beaded curtain disappearing as soon as I stirred. I asked Om if he knew of a spirit that wandered the mansion once night fell. He only smiled and wished me peace.

But this night peace would not come. I tossed on my pillow. Suddenly the curtain parted. He stood before me in his spotless dishdasha, so handsome it hurt my eyes to look at him so I drew the covers over my head. "Asria," he murmured, "it is all right. You may see me."

Slowly I drew down the covers and turned toward him absorbing his faint antiseptic odor. His fingers were long and thin, the fingers of a surgeon. Carefully he approached and perched on the edge of my cot. "Welcome to my home. I did not know they would send me such as you. In the future, please call me Saleh." He smiled and left the room.

I felt as if a warm blanket had been laid upon me. So, this family might come to love me after all. I fell into a deep sleep.

After that, Sir came every night on his return from the hospital. I would wake knowing he was there by the medicinal odor, a fragrance I came to love. "Asria," he would whisper. His delicate fingers touched my shoulder. A soothing balm enveloped me. His voice in the dark glided over me, hypnotizing me to his will. And his will was to have me for his own. Even though he rarely looked my way as I swept the drive for him each morning, I knew he loved me. He told me so when he came to my room and caressed me until I trembled in his arms. I worked in a dream those days smiling as I scrubbed the floors or prepared the morning coffee. I would watch his car leave the drive, hover there until I could no longer hear his motor, praying for his quick return to me each night. It did not matter that he would not look at me in daylight. He looked at me at night. That was enough.

———

Months passed. My love for him overwhelmed me. I thought of him constantly longing for his touch, longing to tell him that I… How should I say it? How should I tell him that I thought…?

"We have been feeding you well," he said one evening as his arms circled my stomach.

I did not know how to reply, so I said nothing until he kissed me there in that special place. Then I had to confess. "Saleh," I whispered, "you have blessed me with your child. She is growing there beneath your kiss."

He rose abruptly as if what I had just said were a sin. In silence, he parted the curtain. I heard his step on the stairs. Then it was as before as if he had never been. Each night I waited for him, but he did not come again. He ordered Om to sweep the drive so he would not have to see me.

As the day of the wedding approached, Fauzia became more irritable. "We are having many guests tomorrow," she said. "The ladies will gather in my bedroom. The men will meet my father downstairs. Then when the contract has been signed by us both, only then will the groom see me. You will prepare the wedding feast in advance, Asria. Do not plan to sleep tonight as the food must be ready by dawn."

I bowed and backed from the room, the weight in my heart greater than that in my womb. Soon my apron would not hide the truth.

That night Saleh came to me in the kitchen as I was preparing the banquet. He stood some distance from me as if I could contaminate him. "I have bought your return ticket." He thrust an envelope on the cutting board. "You will leave tomorrow after my daughter's wedding."

"Saleh," I pleaded, "please allow me to stay. I will have the child in secret. If you wish, I will bury it in the garden beneath a date palm. No one will know. Please allow me…"

He turned to leave.

"I will do anything for you," I called after him. "Spend my life in your service if only…"

The door snapped shut behind him. I wanted to tear the envelope, burn it with the trash, pretend I'd never seen it, that Saleh had not forsaken me. I stared at the cutting board, at the sharp knife that sliced through the bloody chicken and the fish fresh from the sea. I wiped the blade clean and hid it in the largest pocket of my apron. Then, when I was certain the house slept, I mounted the stairs to Fauzia's room. Softly, I opened her door. There she lay in her wedding dress as if she had fallen asleep anticipating the celebration. I parted the veils protecting her. "Fauzia," I murmured to make certain she was still asleep. Then, my hand shaking, I wielded the sharp edge of the kitchen knife toward her heart and plunged it in. Suddenly she stared up at me, her mouth open as if she would scream but no sound escaped. She tried to turn the knife toward me, but I was stronger from my work in the house, the endless months of cleaning and sweeping. She collapsed beneath me, the delicate skin of her chest red as the sash she wore that first morning on my arrival. My body felt numb as if this act had been committed by another being stronger than I. "Toughen up," Rasheed said, and I had. I wiped the bloody blade on her dress. I had killed what was dearest to him. Saleh would have no children now. He would be as bereft as I.

Quickly I descended the stairs and tossed the knife behind some palms hoping a sand drift would bury it. Then I rushed down the path rousting Om who somehow foretold this event.

He called Rasheed on his cell who only agreed to come after I promised him a huge tip. "So," he grinned when he finally arrived, "it did not work out. I could've told you. You're not the first to leave that house. There were many before you."

As we drove to the airport, a dust storm followed us, not the white or yellow dust I had experienced in the past but a whirling black rage. "You have time before your flight?" Rasheed was trying to get ahead of the storm. It was quickly enveloping us.

"Yes, I have time."

"Then I'll pull over and wait for this to pass."

"No don't. Keep going. We'll get stuck in a drift if we pull over."

I hoped the storm would slow the police. Saleh would search for me forever. I knew what my fate would be if he found me. The traffic stalled as we arrived at the airport. Visibility was zero. Inch by inch we approached the entrance guided by the flashing lights of cars in front of us. "Give me my money and get out," Rasheed ordered slinging my suitcase after me. "I should never have agreed to drive you in this mess."

I rushed into the airport and checked my flight for Manila. It was hours before it would leave. My feet felt anchored in cement as I sat on a bench envying the passengers leaving for Addis Ababa, Istanbul, Dubai and other parts of the world where I might find refuge. Suddenly a firm hand gripped my shoulder and forced me from the bench. "You are wanted for questioning," the voice said. I heard it as if through a tunnel. There was still a spattering of blood on my blouse that I could not remove no matter how hard I had tried wetting towel after towel in the Ladies Room.

Soon my wrists were shackled in handcuffs that dug into my flesh until more blood was drawn, my blood this time. And then he arrived in his pure perfection, his face as pale as his dishdasha. "Saleh," I whispered as he joined the policemen. "Saleh please…" But he would not look at me. I had become invisible. He picked a smote of dust from the sleeve of his dishdasha and flicked it in my direction.

The Hanoi Luxury

The Receptionist

WHY IT WAS CALLED Hanoi Luxury I'll never know. Nothing about this hotel was luxurious. It was on Chou Long, a dark street littered with garbage from the shops surrounding it. The roar of motorcycles deafened me. Even in my sleep, I heard them.

I went there searching for a job as their receptionist because I liked the name, Hanoi Luxury. It was the promise of luxury that entranced me, the dream that someday luxury would be mine. I would wake in the morning to the smell of coffee brewing, omelets frying in sweet butter, and fresh squeezed orange juice like on the television that blinked in the lobby. I'd slip into a diaphanous silk and read my newspaper on the love seat or write thank-you notes for the wedding gifts that kept arriving. But the truth was far different.

I walked into the lobby of the Hanoi Luxury that morning and stood trembling at the desk. The lobby was stark, with hardwood benches and full-length mirrors that only reflected the lopsided buildings opposite, the peddlers selling coconuts and bananas, the hungry dogs foraging for scraps. Nevertheless, it smelled new as if the hotel had very few visitors. Maybe that was why they'd advertised for a receptionist, because of their newness. Most other hotels in Hanoi were not so new: the jobs were inherited, passed on to members of the family. To find a position in Hanoi was difficult. I was excited when I saw their ad in the newspaper, "Receptionist Wanted—Computer Skills Necessary—Pay Negotiable."

There was no one in the lobby. It seemed deserted, almost as if it wasn't a real hotel but a set for some arcane movie. I leaned on the water stained counter for support, listening to the drips from the ceiling. New buildings often leaked in Hanoi. They'd been hastily erected with shoddy materials and only passed inspection with bribes. We'd had heavy rains these last few days. The streets were flooded. I was very tired, as I'd walked here from the other side of Hanoi taking a bus as far as it would go, then wading the remainder of the way down the narrow streets that a bus could not penetrate. My white patent shoes were soaked. They were my best shoes, delicate, with straps around the ankle. I'd worn them to impress my interviewer, make him think I had a sense of style important to an upscale hotel, that I could truly represent the luxury of Hanoi Luxury. I hoped my interviewer would understand my dilemma, be compassionate, not reprimand me for my damp blue skirt and white blouse soiled from the mud dripping from rain gutters.

I tried to brush my hair back from my forehead. My bangs had strayed from the band that held them. I thought it important to keep my bangs off my face. With my hair pulled back in a ponytail I looked older, more sophisticated, like the photos of flight attendants on Southern China Airlines that brought foreigners to Vietnam. I would like to be one of those pale attendants, wear that mini skirt, and tie a bright scarf around my neck. I'd even used the whitening powder on the dark face I'd inherited from my Indian mother. With difficulty, I had tried to whiten it so as not to look like a hill peasant. But to no avail, my skin was still the color of cashews roasted in the sun.

The lobby of the Hanoi Luxury was air-conditioned. I shivered in my school blouse. I hated air-conditioning, much preferring the warm breezes outside that calmed me, soothed my nerves, raw from the rain, the long journey here and the impending interview. It was important for me to secure this job, as I had not had work since I finished computer school. I loved the computer, its silence as it traveled the globe. I could go anywhere on my computer. It was my best friend. I loved its sound when I switched it on, the friendly voice telling me I had mail, the endless possibilities as I searched for a friend, a companion, a possible husband. Yes, I wished to marry someday but men were scarce in Hanoi. So many had been killed in the old war, leaving women of child bearing age with no sons or grandsons to propagate the earth. Maybe I will marry my computer, live online for the rest of my life.

I stared at the computer behind the desk, its soft light beckoning me. I had the urge to touch it, settle myself beside its comforting drone, allow myself to bask in its radiance. Slowly I found myself moving behind the desk as if willed to be there. The metal chair seemed comfortable after my long walk. I felt myself relax, adjusted my blouse and skirt, removed my shoes to dry them and was about to take off my wet stockings as well when I heard a shrill voice, like the slap across my cheek my father administered when I failed to find work.

Startled, I jumped from the computer, my stockings around my ankles, my skirt askew as if I'd never bothered to get dressed properly. I staggered as I tried to extricate myself from my computer daze.

"Who gave you permission to touch that computer?" he said in an imperious tone as if warden of a prison.

"I—I couldn't help it. It seemed to need me. No one was here to comfort it so I—I…"

"Are you mental? Comfort a computer? Don't you have any real friends?"

"I—well—I—I guess not. I…"

He looked at me as if I were a computer chip that could be discarded at will. "What are you doing here anyway? You should be in school."

"I was in computer school. I graduated at the top of my class."

"What's that you're wearing then? Looks like a uniform to me. All school girls wear blue and white."

I could not contest his observation. Indeed, it was my school uniform that I was wearing. I'd lowered the neckline and raised the skirt, hoping that with my dress shoes I could fool my interviewer. I had nothing else to wear since I'd graduated. I had two uniforms; one dried while I washed the other.

"Come here," he snapped his fingers as if I were a puppy. And indeed, I felt like one, my hair wet and shaggy as a mane.

I slipped my wet shoes back on, rolled up my stockings and slithered from the desk, wishing I were invisible, that I had never come, that I could leave without notice and never return.

He stood there, his legs planted like rods of steel, a red baseball cap low on his forehead as if he were outside on a field hot with sun. His black eyes glittered. Could he see right through me into the nakedness beneath my clothes? I hung my head trying to avoid his gaze, hoping he couldn't see into my brain as well.

"What brings you here?" he asked not taking his eyes off my body.

"You advertised for a receptionist with computer skills."

"You are much too young for the job. You should be at home helping your mother."

"I have no mother."

"If you are an orphan I will send you back to the orphanage."

"I lived with my father. My mother is with the angels."

"You mean she's dead?"

"She's always with me."

"You mean she's not dead?"

"You might say that."

"You confuse me, girl." He unbuttoned his black blazer and pulled on his tie. It was saffron, the color of spice that my mother sometimes used in her cooking. She had been beautiful. Father had bartered for her as a bride because she was exotic, he said, like her spices, and came from far away, a fairy tale princess. He only became cruel to me after she passed.

"You have a name?"

"Tien," I murmured

"Speak up. If you wish to be a receptionist you must speak up and smile."

I tried to smile. My mouth twitched with the effort.

"Yes, that's better. And do something with your hair. It hangs in your face like a dog's." He yanked my hair back so that my neck strained with the effort to keep my head from detaching.

"And use some of that whitening powder they sell in the market."

"I already have."

"Then the rain must have washed it off." His manicured nails brushed my blouse, ran down my skirt.

"You are more grown up than you appear. Perhaps you will do after all."

"Thank you," I whispered.

"You will report every morning at eight. You will leave when I tell you to. Sometimes guests arrive late at night. I expect you to be here to greet them."

"Your advertisement said pay was negotiable."

"Yes, I will see how effective you are before I make that decision. Let's say, you are on trial."

I nodded agreement.

"Since you were at the top of your class I assume you need no instructions. I'm leaving for my breakfast. You may start now."

"Thank you."

His tight jeans clung to his legs above his high heeled boots. He was a small man with skin smooth from moisturizers and streaked hair greased with pomade. I hoped he would leave quickly so I could retreat behind the desk, relax in the glow of the computer.

"There are no reservations so there should be no one to trouble you. If a room request should arrive refer to the rate chart. If they complain offer a discount, offer anything within reason. But don't let them get away."

He slammed the door so hard the mirrors reverberated. Through the window I watched him descend the concrete steps onto the wet pavement. His narrow hips swayed slightly, his legs agile as an acrobat's. The roar of his motorcycle was a relief. But then it wasn't. If the phone rang what should I say? It rang. I let it ring five times before I picked up. My hands were sweating; my voice caught in my throat. "H-Hanoi Luxury," I stuttered.

"Is Duc there?" A woman's voice trilled.

"Duc?"

"Yes, my husband. Is he there?"

"He's gone for his breakfast. May I take a message?"

"Just tell him his wife called again. And he better answer this time." She clicked off before I could respond.

The morning wore on, and still, Duc did not return. There were no other phone calls, no future reservations. I was afraid he would be angry with me, blame me for the lack of reservations. But I could not invent what was not there, so I diverted myself with soap operas hoping I would also live happily in the end.

Finally, in the early afternoon I heard his motorcycle. It had a strange whine, like a caged beast. His face was flushed, his clothes awry. He smelled of alcohol. I recognized the smell because my father often smelled of it, particularly after a night spent at the many bars in Hanoi that featured women who could be bought for a few drinks.

"Well," he simpered glancing at me sideways as if his eyes had lost focus. "Are we flooded with requests?"

"Not so far. But it's early yet. I'm sure we'll have many reservations later on."

"Could be—could be you'll bring me luck. I haven't had much thus far."

"Your wife called."

"Another bit of bad fortune. Did she leave her usual threat?"

"She said you'd better answer this time."

"I'll think about it after I take a nap."

He looked at me again, his sleepy eyes running over my body like a searchlight.

"I'll be in that little room in back. I won't lock the door in case you'd like to keep me company. The pay is negotiable." He grinned stupidly.

I wanted to run. But where would I go? My father had turned me out this morning when he brought home one of his women. Said it was too crowded with me around. Where would I stay while I sought another position even if one were available, which was doubtful. I felt my body shake with revulsion. Maybe he'll be asleep by now. Maybe he'll lose desire when he sees my body, still undeveloped at the age of eighteen. Maybe he'll allow me to stay on just to answer the calls on the phone, the e-mails on the computer. Maybe…

I felt myself walk towards that room in back, my heart aching, my head throbbing like the rain beating the roof. But I walked anyway. Where else would I go?

The Doorman

I AM PROUD of my new black uniform. "Black will stay clean longer," my brother, Duc, said when he gave me the job as doorman. "What else can I do with you?

What else are you good for with that limp? Just try to stand up straight, Cong, so no one notices."

I try to hide my leg, but that only throws me off balance. Once I fell into the glass door and nearly shattered it. "You're useless," Duc said as he helped me up from the floor.

Duc owns this hotel, the Hanoi Luxury. It is not very luxurious. Duc gave it that name so tourists will come thinking they made a bargain, a luxury hotel for a small price. "Tourists love a bargain," Duc says. "They come from far away, so they will be too tired to cancel their reservation. 'Look how cheap,' I will say to them. 'Where can you find a better deal?'"

Duc must be clever to own so many properties in Hanoi. I don't know how he got so rich while I stayed poor. Even as a child Duc had an eye for money. He searched for lost bills as we walked to school. If I found some between cracks in the pavement, I had to give them to him or he'd punch my face until it looked like a squashed persimmon.

As we grew older, Duc abandoned me to hang with the kids who had more. That wasn't difficult as our family scratched a living from the fish in Truc Bach Lake, selling them to the many restaurants surrounding the water. We played the restaurant game, competing for the best restaurant by spelling its name correctly. Duc always won.

This uniform has bright metal buttons which Duc instructed me to polish every morning. He even gave me a cap. It says, HANOI LUXURY, in big shiny letters that glow in the dark.

Duc expects a big group of students to arrive this evening. They are American, he tells me, so I must be alert, stand at full attention when I open the door. Make certain no one opens it themselves. "We must set an example of courtesy to impress these Americans with the high culture of Vietnam."

Night has fallen. We're still waiting for the Americans. I am standing erect at the door to welcome them. Duc says I must practice standing erect so he will not let me sit even though I've been standing here for hours. "Your leg muscles will not develop if you sit down," he says. So, I stand, wishing they would arrive, so I could finally open and shut this door.

Duc is sporting a checked jacket and black tie tonight. He looks especially keen. Tien, his delicate new hire, sits at the computer as if she's afraid to leave it. I have tried to speak to her but she will not answer. It's almost as if she cannot speak. She begins to tremble when I approach, like a puppy who has lost its mother.

"Tien is very shy," Duc says when I ask about her. Duc does not like me to ask about Tien. It's as if there's some secret he does not wish to share.

At last a bus rumbles to a stop in front of our hotel. It must be the Americans. Several of the girls are tall and blonde. The boys are giant as tree stumps. They yell as they leap from the bus, backpacks crunching their shoulders. They do not help the girls from the bus or carry their luggage as I would do if I did not have to open and close this door.

The girls wear sundresses and short-shorts like they were heading for our beaches rather than the center of Hanoi. Their skin is silky white without the use of the whitening powder they sell in our markets. I can tell this because their arms and legs are white as well as their faces. Only on television have I seen such purity.

Their professor has headphones in his ears. He looks tired, as if this group of unruly students has aged him. He might have been a handsome man if these students had not taken away his youth.

Carefully, I open the door for each one. Some thank me, others do not. It does not matter. I am happy to be opening and closing.

After the professor has checked in his students, I ask Duc if I might retire to my room. It's in the bottom of the hotel next to the kitchen. The smell of fried rice and chicken makes me hungry at night. In the morning the aroma of sour soup makes my stomach grumble for more than the tea and toast Duc prescribes for my portion. I have often asked him if I may be moved upstairs where it's cool and quieter. It's difficult to sleep next to the hot kitchen. And the noise from the streets never stops. I often feel I've never slept at all. Standing at the door, I sometimes sway backwards. "Are you drunk again?" Duc asks. He knows I never drink. On my non-existent salary I can't even afford one beer.

"When we have more guests," Duc says, "I will pay you something. Until then you must be grateful for a place to sleep."

Of course, he's right. Without my brother's generosity I would be out on the street, living with the dogs at night, delivering food to the brothels. I was a delivery boy for years until my bicycle careened into a truck in the early hours of the morning when the fog was just lifting off the lake. My leg was broken in many places. It never healed properly so that now it is difficult to stand at the door. "You are lucky to have such an easy position," Duc tells me. "If you weren't my brother you would be nowhere. Even the dogs despise you."

Of course, Duc is right. "I'm always right," he says each morning when I murmur a complaint because it is raining. My leg always hurts more in the dampness. But I will try never to complain again so my brother will be happy with me.

I have been in my room for several hours now trying to sleep when I hear a great disturbance. Hurriedly, I slip into my uniform and rush upstairs. Several of the boy students are sprawled in the lobby, empty beer cans and liquor bottles cradled in their arms. The girls sit on their laps, kissing them in a shameful manner. I felt myself blush at the sight. I have never had a girl-friend. Perhaps it is my bad leg or my face, which Duc says is a bit like those mongrels that sleep at our door.

Their professor is nowhere in sight. Perhaps he has decided to sleep through this tour whenever possible.

"Cong," the students call, "why weren't you there to open the door for us?"

I rush to the door and stand at attention in case they wish to go out again.

"We're just kidding," they laugh. "We don't want you to open the door for us."

"You don't?"

"No, it's stupid. We can open our own doors. Take a look at our muscle." The boys flex their biceps which indeed are impressive.

"But I wish to open your door. It is my pleasure. It is my job. Duc will be angry. What will he find for me to do if I do not open your door? There is nothing else."

"You must be kidding."

"No, there is nothing for someone like me. My brother is kind enough to give me this job, to allow me to open your door. Please do not tell him that you wish me not to open it."

The students are silent. Such a thing they cannot understand.

The Chef

I WENT TO THE LAKE at sunrise to buy fresh fish for the special lunch that I will prepare for the students. I also bought eggs for their breakfast. I love to visit Truc Bach Lake at this hour. It shimmers in the half-light that is lost by noon when tourists propel paddle boats around its perimeter and fish stop jumping into the nets. I love also the silence of the fishermen along the shore, their concentration on the task at hand. It is this that will bring them the money, the necessary dong to purchase their needs, their sticky rice and tea to greet the dawn. The air smells fresh after the night's rain; fish seem eager to jump into the nets. No one is coughing from the pollution that builds later in the day. Fishermen smile, the silent smile of those who have made a catch, never boisterous as such behavior could turn their luck. Some evil could befall them on their way home, a flat tire on their bicycle as they dodge the traffic, their fish rotting in the sun as they repair it. Such ill can easily befall one in Hanoi. It is a city of strangers now who do not care if they cause injury.

Returning from the lake to the Hanoi Luxury, I avoid the traffic and trod the alleyways hoping no illness befalls me. Men often repair their bicycles in the alleyways, so there is constant danger of slipping on oil or falling over rotting tires or rusty bicycle parts. Duc has cautioned me to be especially careful because of the American students who arrived last night after a long journey. I did not hear the students as I was asleep in the kitchen, guarding my stove from intruders who might steal my fry pans, my colanders and chopping blocks to use in their street kitchens where I could never reclaim them. They would be lost in the confusion of vendors, sold before I could nab the thief and punish him for taking my kitchenware. Duc would surely penalize me. Make me repay him for the stolen goods, dock my salary for months to come. "If you please the students," Duc says, "then your salary will begin."

I will try to please them, make the American egg breakfast that Duc has ordered. Such a breakfast seems strange to me, the weight of the eggs and toast, sausage and bacon are overwhelming, the odors unpleasant. But I will prepare it anyway because it is necessary that I please these students, necessary that I retain my sleeping spot by the stove as the night can bring rain and cold winds off the lake that chill my old bones.

I only have this position because of Duc's generosity. "Uncle," he said, "you are too feeble for this work but you are my uncle so I must care for you. You have no one else. But do not tax my patience, it is limited. Your last days could find you sleeping in the gutter rather than next to the warmth of my stove."

So I am careful not to disturb Duc, but step quietly in his kitchen as if I am invisible. As if the breakfast were produced by magic, a miracle breakfast for the students.

I hear them now on the stairs. Their step is heavy, voices loud, like radio at full volume. I do not understand what they are saying. Their English is different from that I learned in school. It has lost the resonance that I prefer, the musical sound of the syllables.

I am wearing my white chef's hat and coat to impress them. Tien washed and starched it for me yesterday. Duc would not pay the laundry. "Tien will take care of it," he said. Tien is the hotel's receptionist. She is skilled at the computer, but Duc has her performing many other tasks as well. If anything goes wrong in the hotel, he screams at Tien. She shudders like a palm frond before the storm, tries to hide her face in the computer, but Duc lashes out until she pleads for him to stop.

Last night Tien said Duc accused her of stealing dong from a student's wallet. How could she have done such a thing when she had been with Duc through the night in the little room in back that I had hoped would be a prayer room with an altar where we could pay homage to our ancestors, light candles, leave sweet meats and fruit. But Duc said that was foolish. "Your ancestors do not remember you, so why waste time remembering them?"

When I woke this morning, Tien was standing by my stove shivering. I tried to comfort her. She is such a sweet child. I am pleased she confides in me. I wish I could protect her from Duc. But no one can be protected from his wrath. We are his servants and must do his bidding.

I am standing at attention now awaiting orders. The kitchen and dining room are spotless. Tien and I have washed the floors. Cong, the doorman, has set the table with clean linens. I have set out pans of sausage, grilled tomatoes, fried potatoes and onion. Also, I have prepared the false orange juice from Tang, brewed coffee and Lipton tea in the little bags.

The students stumble into the dining room still half asleep from the journey, hair uncombed, faces unwashed, shorts and T-shirts torn as if they are street people. Tien has told me such attire is common in America. She has seen it on her computer.

I smile at them, my best smile, try to hide my broken molar and rotting incisors. When my salary begins I will see the dentist. I would like to have a new, shiny set of teeth that I could take out at night, brush carefully in the morning and replace them to smile at the sunrise on my way to the lake. Perhaps then some vendors might smile back and I would not feel so lonely on my journey.

I stand with my eggs now awaiting the students' requests. Palm oil sizzles in the pan. However, I do not understand their orders. The line gets longer. The students start laughing among themselves, shuffling feet, making strange signs to each other. Breaking some eggs into the fragrant oil, I show them to the students hoping they will tell me what to do. But it is no use. They do not want my broken eggs. They do not want my bacon or sausage, my grilled tomatoes. "Cereal," they call. "Don't you have any Frosted Flakes or Cheerios?" Such foods I am not familiar with. In my chef training no mention was made of Cheerio or Frosty Flake.

Suddenly Duc is standing before me, his face like a boiled lobster, his fists clenched. He is wearing a snappy red sports coat, red trousers and black shirt. His hair is slicked back with the grease they sell in the market. His skin smells of lavender oil.

"Uncle," he fumes, "why did you not buy the cereal on your way from the lake? I told you the students need their Cheerio and Frosty Flake."

"You—you did not tell—." But I think it better not to contradict Duc, so I say it was too early. The market was not yet open. But that does not calm his anger. He grabs the pan of eggs dumping them on the floor.

"Are you too old to understand anything?" he screams.

I hang my head, slump my shoulders trying to grow smaller as I sink to my sleeping spot beside the stove. I hunch down like a dog hoping to avoid the blow from his raised fists. But I need not have been concerned. The students rally. Surrounding Duc they force him to retreat. His fists unclench. A twitch of fear tightens his lips as he stares at the students in bewilderment, at the objection of the Americans to his behavior. Turning, he slips on the stairs which are still slick from Tien's washing. "Tien," he yells, but stops as the students move in closer, their faces grim. Muttering to himself like the crazies who wander our streets, Duc clings to the railing and hobbles his way from the kitchen, slamming the door behind him.

I kneel to clean up the mess. "Here, Uncle," several of the students volunteer, "let us help you."

I am hoping the students will stay at HANOI LUXURY a very long time.

The Flowers

"COME IN AND SMELL THE FLOWERS," I called when I saw the tourists rush from the buses to be first in line to see our Revered Uncle. I have his likeness at the entrance to my Water Closet. They cannot miss Uncle Ho as they push open the wooden door, still sodden from Hanoi's last storm. I know they all have to come here eventually. No one can avoid the flowers.

I have been in this dank cave since before dawn. I took the early bus from the countryside. It was the only bus that would bring me to the Mausoleum before the crowds arrived. I was hours early but better than being late. I could sit on my box outside my WC and watch the sun rise over Ba Dinh Square, gradually lighting the granite of the Mausoleum, soft rays of rose and gold. Inside I knew Uncle was resting peacefully.

One day I bribed the guards to get a small glimpse of dear Uncle before the mobs made that impossible. I brought him gold chrysanthemums that I purchased at the bus stop. They were too expensive, but I bought them anyway. I would make it up somehow when the tourists came, when they could no longer avoid my flowers.

The guards were half asleep at their posts, white uniforms crisp as the rice pancake I hid in my pocket. "Auntie," they murmured through half closed lids, "what have you brought us?"

I slipped them the pancake I'd baked before I left my village and the fried banana wrapped in palm leaf I'd buried in my shawl. They were grateful to have their day begin with such delicacies as usually they had only sticky rice and tea for breakfast.

I tiptoed through the dim coolness, up marble staircases, along polished corridors to the middle tier of the three stories. Uncle Ho's chamber was dark except for a pale light that came from the shining catafalque of black marble. Dressed in a plain tunic and sandals, he rested within the glass-framed sarcophagus. Removing my shoes, I approached with care. No one except the guards must know I have been here.

I stood for a long while gazing at the smooth skin of his face, ageless now beneath the sheen of glass.

We are told Uncle believed in his people. The poor were always in his thoughts. I am certain this is true, as he himself lived a simple life, avoiding the excess that can come with riches.

"Uncle Ho," I whispered, "be with me today. Make many come to my flowers. Let them leave large tips in my basket so I may buy a big catfish from the vendors at Truc Bach Lake. I wish my grandchildren should not go hungry tonight. They are so small, Uncle. Their parents are no longer here to guide them. They are dead from the disease, the unmentionable one. I must care for their children now, be father and mother. It is not easy as I am old, soon too withered to work, like a dried grape on a forgotten vine. I pray, Uncle, you hear me."

I heard a click in the hall, the guard getting ready to make his visitors count for the day. His cough warned me. I fell to my knees before Uncle, bowed three times and kissed the floor before I went to my WC. I had cleaned it good before I returned to my village last night, locked it tight with a double padlock so no thieves could steal my mops, pails, brooms, soaps or whatever else they found inside. There was nothing they would not take to sell on the Black Market.

The guards smiled as I left, bits of pancake and banana between their teeth. "Smell a flower for me, Auntie," they laughed. "Make it a big one."

I ignored them in their stiff uniforms and blank gaze. They had nothing to do all day but stand like statues, handsome and young, admired by all the visitors while I, in my faded dress—whose true color I can no longer recall—and skin coarse as unpolished granite, hurried down the steps like a passing shadow.

The sun dazzled me when I returned to the daylight. A faint wind brushed the feathery leaves of the bamboo groves that cornered the Mausoleum. I drank in the sweet scent of jasmine, frangipani, and dog-rose, knowing that the only flowers I would smell the rest of the day were those of the Water Closet, the acrid odor of the Eastern toilet and the foul smell of the Western. I would rush to clean them before the next customer arrived. "Come in and smell the flowers," I would smile hoping their humor was good and they would laugh at the joke I played on them.

Today a tourist arrived wearing shorts and a halter. Her upper arms flapped when she raised them to tug at her black pony tail held tight by a rubber band. Her hair was so black I was certain she must have used the special dye so popular in the market. I have used some myself from time to time in a vain effort to conceal the gray that has gradually overtaken my head, turned it into dull streaks that I tie up beneath a straw sunhat so no one can see how my once beautiful hair has changed.

It offended me to see one so old dressed like a girl. It was improper, an insult to Uncle Ho who was always modest in his appearance and expected the same from his people. This woman should be sent back to her hotel on the next bus, told to cover herself if she wished to view our revered leader. Would she visit her White House, the home of her President, dressed in such a manner?

The woman tried to pass me by without putting any dong in my basket. I stood in her path to prevent her from entering. I could see she was desperate by the way she shifted from left foot to right.

"I don't have the correct change," she said.

"What do you have?"

"Only this," she pulled a 500,000 dong note from her overloaded backpack.

"Give it to me. I will have change when you are done smelling my flowers."

She did not smile but ran inside to the first closet that was vacant.

"There is no paper," she called

"Wait-wait I will bring some."

I went to my cabinet where the paper was locked. It was expensive. I tried to avoid providing it, hoping the customer would have some in her purse. I knew tourists were told to carry some for such emergencies. Of course, if they would learn to use the Eastern toilet, clean themselves with soap and water, all this paper would not be necessary.

I got two small sheets and brought them to her. "Here," I reached beneath the door viewing her long toenails, painted red like the whores in Old Town. Her white sandals were caked with the mud I would have to scrape from the floor when she left.

Her chipped fingernails reached for the paper. "Is that all you have?"

"That is your portion. There is extra charge for more."

"I need more."

I went to my cabinet and got another sheet, slipping it beneath the door. "This should do."

But it was still not enough, so I brought her many sheets until my stock was empty. I would have nothing for my other customers, and it was early in the day.

No one will laugh, no tips in my basket, no catfish for my grandchildren or sole or fried rice with pork and mushrooms.

She came from the toilet adjusting the zipper on her shorts and stood waiting for her change. I knew she was new to Vietnam otherwise she would not have given me 500,000 dong, equal to 30 dollars American. She had not examined our currency. Maybe she was stupid. Maybe she was rich and did not care. But I cared for my grandchildren. They would have catfish tonight and sole with fried rice as well to fill their aching stomachs.

I went to my money drawer and opened the padlock. I withdrew many small dong, worth very little, about $5.00 American. They fluttered in her hand.

"Your money is so pretty," she smiled at last. "I love the pastels." She did not bother to count it as she stuffed it into her pack.

Before I return to my village, I will visit Chua Mot Cot, the one pillar pagoda and thank Quan Am, our Lady of Mercy, for this gift. I will climb the Lotus Tower to kneel before her bed of lotus blossom. I will burn many joss sticks, smell deep the sandalwood and make a large donation for those who are less fortunate.

The Driver

I WAIT FOR THEM in the alley behind Phan Ngu Lao street, around the corner from Nha Bac Co, the National Museum of Vietnamese History.

"What's that?" They always ask, pointing sweaty fingers at the museum's octagonal tower, gaping at its brilliance, shielding their eyes from its golden reflection as if it were a mirage.

"I will wait for you," I call as they plod the steps to the archway, entering the cool depths of the museum. I offer to be their guide but they do not respond, probably thinking I know nothing of the museum and that sleeping in my trishaw has made me stupid. And maybe it has. Who else would be crazy enough to cycle this city year after year, until their bones crack with fatigue. But I have done this work as long as I can remember and so must continue to do it. It's a sunset occupation and will not exist much longer. Tourists prefer the comfort of cars and buses, particularly when the rains come. But the work is in my blood and my father's before me.

I know this museum as well as I know my own body. I've trod its stone steps a hundred times or more, cooling myself on a balcony or on a slow day, settling for a brief nap on the great couches of the second floor where tourists rarely come, the effort of climbing being too much for them after the mid-day heat. I feel safe next to Buddha, our god of enlightenment, with eleven faces and forty-two arms to hold my prayers. "Protect me Buddha," I implore, closing my eyes. Such is the power of this god that when I wake I feel strong again, ready to face the traffic, to cycle to Saigon if need be. I would like to see Saigon. All I have ever seen is Hanoi. Maybe that is best. I hear there is danger in Saigon, but nevertheless I hope someday to cycle there, to pack my meager belongings and head south. I must do this before I die.

There's a beautiful screen on the second floor of this museum that inspires my dreams. It has three panels of wood and oyster decorated with landscapes, citadels, horses and noblemen. They say it was influenced by the art of the Chinese. Everything elegant is said to be Chinese rather than French. But it was the French who constructed this building. It remained their consulate until 1910. We like to think we have rid ourselves of the French but that is a myth. We buy their bread in the markets, long crisp baguettes, fragrant in the heat rising off Truc Bach Lake where my favorite French bakery is located.

You may have noticed my shack in your walks around the lake. It's near the little bridge that separates the lake into two unequal portions. Soon, I'm afraid my shack will no longer exist. I'll be forced to spend the night cramped in my trishaw. I wake every morning now to the roar of machinery erecting another high rise, as if the dying lake were a glorious place to be. As if there were no dead fish in its waters or garbage from the vendors along its shore.

I cover my head with a bag from the bakery to blot out the sound, to give me a few minutes more rest before I cycle to the museum. The machines are like monsters from nightmares ravishing the lake shore. For years I've been allowed to dwell in this cardboard shack, have been respected by passersby. No thieves have come in the night because there is nothing to steal. Sometimes the would-be thief has left me a baguette or an orange and occasionally a banana as well.

At one time, when I was younger, I could cycle more miles in a day than my body will allow at present. Then I could afford a coffee from the vendors, sit on a straw mat along the shore and offer my services to the tourists, but no more. My throat is dry now. It aches for the taste of coffee on my tongue, its aroma flooding my nostrils.

I've been warned by the authorities that my shack will soon be gone, will slide into the lake one night when I'm asleep. I'll wake in the morning chilled by the fog rising off Truc Bach Lake, no roof over my head, no coffee or baguette to nourish me. Oh Buddha, I pray again, save me from the machines, protect me in the darkness.

When I open my eyes, the sun has begun to fade. The light inside the vast halls of Hebard's architectural masterpiece is soft and comforting. I glide down the staircase past the ancient lime pots that served for mixing ceremonial betel, the Chu Nam books of geography and poetry containing the oldest map of Hanoi. Holding my breath, I hurry past Siva, the Hindu god of destruction, hoping I can escape his gaze.

The security guard is my nephew, so he lets me pass. "Uncle," he says, "dream well and often." He smiles at me, a lopsided smile, as his face was scarred in childhood. A gang of boys had battered him until he could hardly breathe. I found him lying still and helpless beside the lake and nourished him back to health. His parents had died the year before from the unmentionable disease that plagues our city.

I go back outside to the alley where my trishaw is parked. A small boy waits for me. He's thin as a rice noodle and just as slippery. His palm is outstretched. He has guarded my trishaw while I napped. I place a few dong in his hand, not enough even to buy a baguette, but he's grateful. He's a street boy who has eluded the authorities. He should be in school. It's compulsory and free. When I was a child, this was not so. I had to learn by myself. My parents were illiterate. I tell him this. I tell him education is a great blessing. But he will not listen, darting into the alley when the police arrive on trucks to harass the unlicensed vendors, mostly women from the villages selling their surplus crops to support their families.

I wait in the shade of the alley for a long time before a couple passes. The man beckons me from the shadows. I climb down from my trishaw and rush to him. "Hotel Hanoi Luxury," he mutters.

"Hanoi Luxury?"

"Near Truc Bach Lake."

"Yes-yes," I say pretending I know his hotel. There are so many on little side streets, new ones all the time.

"60,000 dong." I blow some leaves from the seat of my vehicle.

"30,000," he counters. I see he relishes bargaining.

"50,000," I answer thinking his hotel is near the lake, so I will be almost home when I deliver them.

"40,000," he replies nudging his wife in the opposite direction.

"Okay-okay," I call after them hoping he'll tip me much more when he sees how hard I must pedal to insure their safety, how careful I must be not to collide with cars and buses, not to injure tourists crossing against the light.

He turns to his wife and gives her a sly smile. With effort, he boosts her into my cab. Her haunches are wide, like slabs of beef hanging in the market. She's not young, not old, but that indeterminate age that coincides with bleached hair and makeup so thick it only emphasizes the wrinkles it is intended to conceal.

I smile at them. "Hanoi Luxury," I repeat, edging carefully into the traffic.

"Would you like to go by Old Town?" I call back. "I can show you the historic house, N87 Ma May Street where the tradesmen purchased bamboo and rattan. You can go inside, see how they lived back then."

"I don't think so." His wife suppresses a yawn.

"Or I could take you to see The Water Puppets. The puppeteers stand up to their hips in water telling old tales. You will laugh. They are very funny."

"Yeah, well maybe next time." He brushes a fly from the tip of his sunburned nose. "Damn insects'd eat ya alive."

"I think maybe you are tired. We could see some of the original houses now preserved for massage."

"Legit?" he shouts over the traffic.

"Who's to say?" I smile back at him.

"What do they charge?"

"You can bargain."

His wife looks straight ahead; her gaze deliberate as if this question had arisen many times before. "Take us to the hotel," she snaps. "We can see Old Town another time."

"Okay-okay," I laugh.

She looks pleased as we pass the silk shops. "Let's come back tomorrow. I bet they can make me something wonderful."

"You're wonderful enough." He squeezes her swollen fingers bursting with amethyst and emeralds.

"You're hurting me," she whimpers.

We round the corner only to find the road blocked by police, a bicycle accident. The woman lies on the ground, her basket of fruit rolling in every direction. No one gathers the fruit. Perhaps they are afraid the police will accuse them of stealing. The motorcycle she collided with is parked at the curb, its driver stricken. The vendors pay no attention, keep frying bananas, shining shoes, selling maps of the city, pirated copies of *Lonely Planet*. These accidents are a daily occurrence like a change in the weather or a forecast of more strife between North Vietnam and South despite the union of the country.

The ambulance arrives crushing fruit in its path. I steer us into a side street. "Good thinking." The man pats my shoulder. "I thought we'd be there forever."

"Okay-okay?" I smile back.

"Okay," he wipes dust from his sun glasses, placing them gingerly back on his sun burned nose.

I cycle on, sweat dripping into my eyes even though my straw hat provides ample shade. There's a milky veil over my eyes these days that I must take care of. Perhaps on a slow day, I'll visit the clinic, wait in the hall for my number to be called only to be informed I'm old, such eyes belong to the elderly. There is no cure.

We finally reach the lake. I knew we were there long before I turned the corner. I could smell the fish, the rotting chicken, dregs of coffee from morning's breakfast.

"Close enough." He taps my shoulder.

"I can take you right to your doorstep," I reply, thinking that would earn me more dong.

"No, close enough. We're just around the corner." He climbs from my cab helping his wife descend. I jump down to help her also. As I said, she's a big woman pushing the extremities of the seat. Her husband is small and sprightly. It must be hard to have your way with this woman.

He removes a huge pile of dong from his leather wallet. I could see it is genuine leather, prized in Vietnam and costly. His wife looks on with interest, silently counting the dong as he unfolds the pastel notes and slips them into my hand. I recount them and smile, "40,000?"

"Yes," as we bargained.

"So we did. But you see the distance I have taken you, clear across the city with no mishaps. You could easily have lost your lives on such a journey. Is there no reward for such diligence?"

"A bargain is a bargain." He propels his wife toward their hotel.

"May Siva reward you!" I call after him. Clouds darken the sky with a distant rumble of thunder.

But he does not turn. It's as if I never existed, never cracked my bones to avoid the cars and buses, cabs and bicycles that might have ended their holiday.

I felt tired, wanted only to rest myself, return to my shack and lie on the cardboard floor with a market bag over my head, blot out this journey, return to my daydreams with Buddha holding my prayers in his forty-two arms.

Mounting my trishaw, I head toward my shack on the other side of the lake. "Coffee?" the vendors call, "mangoes, sweet coconut, banana?"

I was too tired to eat. Even with the dong in my pocket, I had little interest in their wares. The 40,000 would buy me a few baguettes maybe, an orange or two and a coffee if I'm careful.

I rounded the lake where my shack stood on the other side of the little bridge, opposite the house with the chained dog that growled as I rode by, his fangs ready to tear me apart for his dinner.

Carefully, I examined the shoreline, not seeing anything that resembled my shack. I rode closer to the machines and motioned to the driver who paid no attention. Finally, I parked my trishaw under one of the few trees still standing and stood in the path of the monster. He screeched to a halt cursing me. "You crazy?" he yelled. "You want kill yourself?"

"Where is my shack? What have you done with it?"

"It floats in lake. We warned you. Jump in. Maybe you save it."

He started his motor. The roar deafened me. He rolled his machine in my direction. I would have jumped in only I couldn't swim, and the lake was foul. Surely, I'd catch some disease that would end my usefulness.

For hours I watched the lake for signs of my shack, for remnants floating on the silt. Darkness approached. Lights glimmered from hotels on the other side of the water. The milky veil covering my eyes developed a halo that blinded me. I climbed back into my trishaw. "Buddha protect me," I prayed. "Let me rest in your arms." In the morning I'll cycle to Saigon.

The Hairdresser

I WAS IN MY ROOM behind the shoe shop where the electric wire is fastened to the telephone pole when the call came. "Hurry Phuoc," the Sofitel's receptionist screeched, "it's an American."

I'd never seen an American at the Sofitel. Few Americans have visited Hanoi since the big war many years ago, before my birth even. I had learned something about it in school, how Americans bombed our women and children. How, for that reason, we should hate Americans. Indeed, many of us still do. But as I see so few of them, it's difficult to hate what isn't there. Besides, Americans are known for their money. Money is something we desperately need in Hanoi. Northern Vietnam is not like the South, like Saigon, which prospers with American handouts. I hear they have huge department stores there with glitzy windows and elegant jewelry for sale, French perfume and American appliances.

I wish I could transfer my trade south. But what trade? There is none. I sit at the Sofitel waiting for a real customer, someone who is not Vietnamese, whose hair is not black, who does not wish a black dye job for their graying temples, someone who resembles the women in *ELLE*, the blondes and red heads, pale brunettes or silver whites ...

Yes, I have become depressed of late, wondering why I ever took up such an unstable occupation. All I had to do was look around, and I could see what my future would be. But I did not look around I looked inward instead, burying myself in the dream world of fashion magazines, and in my sleep cutting and coloring the beautiful models in their pages, only to encounter the next morning another coarse head of black hair that needed shaping. But now, with this call, perhaps my life is changing. Perhaps I will run to the Sofitel and lines of Americans will wait, their silky tresses longing for the touch of my coconut shampoo, my freshly sharpened scissors, my color brush, and comb. I will mold their heads into the latest fashion, long and straight hair like the anchors on American TV or short and wild like some of the stars in Hollywood magazines. My name will be linked with theirs. "Hair designs by Phuoc," they will read. My assistants will be many. I will choose them carefully from those who are waiting to audition, exhibiting their skills on mannequins before I deign to hire them. They will call me Monsieur with a Parisian accent, tremble slightly as they cut and color to my specifications ...

The morning now is overcast. A hint of rain silvers the palms as I run past Truc Bach Lake, dodging the vendors, hopscotching the banana leaf mats set with red plastic cups and chopsticks in hope of customers. On another day I might stop for a French baguette, sweet pineapple and green tea but not this morning. A putrid smell rises from the lake, which is often used as a toilet by the itinerant homeless. I try not to breathe deeply, to take short puffs of air so I do not infect my lungs. Much of our population has the lung disease that comes from the stench, the foul pollution…

I run on, passing the Indian restaurant. An aroma of curry spices the brooding air. The French café is grinding fresh beans for morning café au lait, and the tattoo parlor has just repainted their sign in brilliant reds and purples. In a distant temple, the monks are busy with morning incantations as they kneel before the golden Buddha and his frightening protectors, wielding knives and swords should anyone dare to challenge their god's sanctity. Wafted by the breeze, their voices soothe my anxiety. I am afraid the American will have left by the time I arrive.

I puff my way up the hill, passing fruit carts of overripe durian that smell like French cheese kept too long in the cupboard. I dodge the incessant stream of motorcycles and autos that honk me deaf. Clouds gather overhead as if to warn me. And then the rain, light at first, comes down in torrents. People rush by with newspapers over their heads. Vendors cover their carts with plastic bags from the market and hide beneath. But there is no place to hide as the rain pelts me, destroying my freshly ironed shirt, my shined shoes and pomaded hair. I resemble a sewer rat and suddenly wish I could join them down below the gutter. Why did I ever choose this unrewarding career? Why didn't I sense my disappointment years ago when, at the age of eight, I dressed paper dolls and wore my mother's skirts for dress up, sneaking her makeup when she wasn't looking. But she thought I was a doll and never warned me about the possibility of a disastrous future in a trade dominated by females.

Finally, I reach the hilltop and see the Sofitel in all its pretended elegance. The doorman has disappeared. Behind the glass, clerks don sweaters as if the rain were inside instead of out, hoping it will dissipate by lunch time so they can buy fried peanuts and bananas from their favorite vendors.

I slip on the puddle outside the revolving door, splashing mud on the edge of my blue jeans. But I am beyond caring. I shake myself off inside the door, resembling the shaggy animals on the street. Peering in the window of the hair salon, I take a deep breath before I enter. In a soft bamboo chair sits an elderly woman. She sips from a white ceramic cup of coffee. In her lap is the latest issue of *ELLE*. Her feet are encased in gold stilettos beneath a leather skirt, which is much too short for a woman of her age, and a pink silk blouse from which her breasts protrude like mounds of marshmallows. White hair bushes from her head in strange tufts as if she's teased it into this bizarre coiffure. What will I do with her, I think. What in the name of Buddha will I do?

Grabbing a hairdryer, I hide behind a screen and blast it at my jeans, which cling to my hips in a rather provocative fashion. Well, maybe that isn't all that bad. Stepping from behind the screen, I approach her, smiling. "I apologize for keeping you waiting, Madam. The rain you see … and I point outside to the torrent splattering the windows.

"No problem," she replies, "I'm staying at this hotel."

"You're staying here?" Foreigners usually book the Sheraton or one of the fancy hotels near the embassies.

"Yes, everything else was taken."

"I hope you enjoy your visit. If Obama is elected relations between our countries will surely improve."

She smiles in agreement.

"I would like to visit the U.S. one day," I say. "I would like also to see Canada too. How much flying time between California and Vancouver? Is it like maybe the same as between Hanoi and Saigon?"

She looks puzzled. Perhaps my Viet accent has kept her from understanding, so I change the subject to something more immediate. "What can I do for you?" Lifting a lock of her hair, I display my scissors.

She shakes her head in a negative fashion.

"Color?" I ask, hoping she'll say yes, as that's an expensive process.

"Weave," she says.

I bring her a color chart. She points to the color she wants woven through her white, a dark brown, similar to a zebra coat. I think she would be better off with a full coloring, a gorgeous red or platinum blonde so I could display my expertise. Weaving is difficult; each lock separated from the others, then rolled in foil, followed by a tedious heat process.

I smile. "Of course," I say, but tremble inside. I've never done a weave. Such a thing is not popular with Vietnamese. In fact, it is almost unknown. You occasionally see a teenager with a shock of purple, red, or gold but a full weave, never. Maybe I can talk her out of it. Maybe I can show her models with white hair dyed red or blonde. Politely, I show her some photos. "Would you prefer…" I offer.

She shakes her head impatiently. It's obvious she wants me to get on with the job. I dare not delay any longer. She could easily escape; visit a foreign salon where they were used to Americans, performed weaves day in and day out. If I am successful she will recommend me. I might have a chance at stardom after all.

"Come." I place a fresh gown over her clothing, carefully snapping it in place. Then I slip in a CD of some soft Vietnamese love ballads to soothe her as I get my color pot ready, mixing the zebra brown that she requested. Gently, I part her hair, painting some strands in zebra stripes, leaving others white. Rolling the stripes in foil, I set her under the dryer with her copy of *ELLE* and her coffee. "Voila," I say, and imitate the little twirl I'd seen in hot French movies.

She looks pleased as she begins to doze beneath the warmth of the dryer. Nervously, I hover about her, wondering how my zebra will look with her new coiffure. When the timer rings I remove the dryer, unroll her hair and lead her to the basin. Gently bending her head back as if she were one of the dolls I played with as a child, I shampoo her hair, adjusting and readjusting the water temperature until she smiles. The brown dye washes into the basin. I'm soon afraid no color will be left. Lifting her head, I tie a towel around it and lead her back to my station. Removing the towel, I am aghast. The dark stripes bled into the white, so there is no definition. She resembles a zebra confused in the womb of its mother. I am ready to apologize only I don't know what to say, so I stand there smiling as I run the blow dryer over her head.

She smiles back. "Just what I wanted," she whispers, admiring herself in the mirror, "nothing too defined, a bit abstract, like a Rothko maybe.

I don't know this Rothko, so I say nothing, only smile brighter when she slips a big tip into my sweating hand.

Hanoi Hangout

DON'T TRY TO FIND US. We're not your usual gym. There are no neon lights, no windows revealing the rusty equipment, broken stair climbers and sagging bikes. No air conditioning either even though the Hanoi sun is blistering, trees drooping, bushes begging for water. It'll soon come, I think. Soon the monsoons will hit us. Our streets will flood, bicycles collide, trishaws skid to a stop, their occupants drenched.

Today heat sits like a mantle on the city, unmoving, uncaring for the comfort of its population. But still I love it and would not wish to live anywhere else. I'm intoxicated by the smell of frying bananas, sweet pineapple, roasting peanuts and coffee. If I could have breakfast all day, I would. Who needs anything more than a demitasse of rich French espresso accompanied by a fresh baguette? On Sunday I'll indulge this fantasy. Today I must restrict myself to the energy drinks we sell here, the vitamin rich formulas we market, proclaiming their beneficial effects even though we've yet to see any amazing results. I've been drinking them since I was hired, mostly because they're free for employees. And I can't resist anything free. Neither can anyone else in Hanoi. We're a city of beggars, of pretenders. Just look at my shoes, Adidas, yes? No, they're not Adidas; they're pretend Adidas, knockoffs. Do you think with my non-existent salary I could afford the real thing?

I call myself a Personal Trainer, it's impressive. In truth, I'm training only myself. None of our clients can afford a Personal Trainer, most of them don't even know what that is. They were trained in the streets avoiding cars and motorcycles. They learned how to jump, to swing over a fence with a stolen watermelon tucked beneath an elbow. Their personal training was natural, part of daily life in a city where the traffic never slows for a pedestrian.

It's still early. I've been up since 5 a.m., when we open to accommodate office workers, paper shufflers trying to maintain a minimum of muscle to impress their girlfriends. I'll be here until 10 p.m. when we close for the night.

When I arrive, I open all the windows to catch any breeze that might sneak through the alley. We're secluded in an old courtyard filled with forgotten newspapers and yesterday's trash. Our building is ripe for condemnation. The walls are crumbling, the stairway to the fourth floor where the weight machines are, unsteady. I warn people to be careful climbing, to cling to the banister in case the steps should collapse. It's possible that at one time this building was a residence for dignitaries. At least that's what I prefer to think. It's in the heart of Hanoi. What could be better? There are traces of grandeur, a sculpted stairwell here, an engraved tile there. I've tried to obtain the history of this building, but no one has any knowledge. Perhaps that's just as well. It makes living in its remains easier, opens its former splendor to the imagination.

The third floor is reserved for aerobics, the lower two for offices and restrooms. The women will soon arrive clad in their skimpy outfits revealing every imperfection. They're so unlike their mothers, shrouded in long skirts and sun hats.

"Good morning, Ladies." I smile as they trudge up to the third floor, while I blast a Michael Jackson CD to get their blood pumping. I shout over the lyrics. I love to shout; it's exhilarating. The women respond, breathing in time to the music, their flesh jiggling inside their leotards. "That's it," I yell, "that's it. C'mon now, let's go. One-two-three-four." We do jumping jacks, swing our legs, grind our buttocks, twirl and whirl for an hour. They're sweating, heaving, some sink to the floor to recover. And then I sell them bottled water with French labels, energy drinks from America, and Nestle's chocolate. I make a small commission on each item. Sometimes it's enough to buy a kite for my brother. My brother is two years older than I am, but has the mentality of a child. "It was a punishment," Ma said because he was born out of wedlock. So was I for that matter. But Ma claimed she'd been punished enough and that's why the gods allowed me to be normal.

Flying kites is my brother's only pleasure. I choose kites that are especially colorful with designs that delight him, dragons and monsters, spiders erupting from the sky... We fly them on Sundays when the gym is closed. Ma climbs with us to the rooftop. She brings a picnic basket so we can pretend we're somewhere else, an imperial park maybe, or the beautiful beaches we've seen on television. Ma seems happy then. Her face glows with pleasure as she feeds my brother spiced tofu on rice, a Sunday favorite. My mother is still in her prime, still able to bear more children, that's why it's my duty to protect her, guard her against the unwanted advances of adventurers. There are many such men in this city. And vulnerable women like my mother are a prime target. Offer them a new dress or shoes for their kids and they succumb.

It's early afternoon now, a quiet time. The ladies have left for lunch. Only a few hangers on remain, the ones who watch TV all day instead of exercising. They buy a year's pass, which entitles them to sit and chat as if this were some kind of country club. I don't discourage this, as they purchase energy drinks for their energy-less existence. They love to watch melodramas, the fantasy lives of those richer and more glamorous than themselves. Perhaps we all live in a fantasy world here, imagining our bodies growing stronger and more flexible when there is little evidence that that is so.

I'm wearing clean white shorts today. Ma laundered them over the weekend. My T-shirt reads HANOI

HANGOUT in large black letters so no one can miss them as I bicycle to work, avoiding the main thoroughfares, preferring the back alleys where women hang clothes to dry, calling to each other as if telephones were non-existent, as if this were a medieval city, a relic of forgotten history. I try to dodge the drips from socks and sweaters, jeans and jackets, sometimes arriving at my destination with damp hair and soggy socks. But still I prefer the safety of the alleys to the bedlam beyond.

Across the steaming courtyard, I view the temple. It must be cool in the interior. I'd love to be there right now, kneeling at the foot of the Golden Buddha. I'd stay there until nightfall, until the lights of the city blazed my way home. I'd sleep on the roof watching the stars retreat behind a cloud, waiting for the monsoon rains to cool me.

Suddenly, from the corner of the courtyard, I see them approaching, one very tall boy and two girls, all of them pale, white as the flour in my mother's cupboard. I wonder what they're doing here, these interlopers dressed in smart running shoes with American labels, Nike and New Balance. The girls have hair the shade of sunshine with frosted lips and eyes like amethysts. I could fall in love with these girls if the boy were not so present, so large, like an overgrown palm tree making me feel small and insignificant. I hear them enter, climb the rickety stairs, remarking in American English on its irregularity, their tone nasal and flat as the rice pancakes Ma fried for breakfast, peanut oil oozing from the edges.

I say nothing, wait for them to greet me, to offer some dong for admission. But they only proceed to the machines, taking over the gym as if it were their own. Their bodies are sculpted and lean. Obviously, they've been working out in the incredible athletic clubs in the U.S.A. I've seen them advertised in magazines, as sterile and sleek as their inhabitants.

They seem oblivious of me as if I'm merely another piece of deteriorating equipment. Their confidence is intimidating, so I hang with the hangers-on and observe them, waiting for them to complete their workout before I approach with the bill for the use of this facility. The girls spend a full hour on the treadmill while keeping time to the music on their headphones. The boy is absorbed with the weights, puffing as he heaves ever heavier barbells, while admiring himself in the full-length mirror. I envy his muscles as they bulge from his red T-shirt, LA FITNESS emblazoned on his chest. No matter how much I exercise, my muscles remain diminutive, like crab apples rather than the full ripe ones they sell in the markets, wrapped in plastic, imported from the States.

I surf the channels to find a station I enjoy while I wait for them to finish. Gradually I become mesmerized by a rerun of Orange County. Perhaps that's where these kids are from. They resemble the mannequin features of the stars, their Botoxed beauty.

The afternoon wears on and still they're here. I begin to drowse, am startled awake by a commercial and drowse again only to hear their voices in the courtyard. For a moment I think I must be dreaming, that someone switched channels on the television. But no, it's them, loud and clear. I rush to the stairwell and shout for them to stop, jumping the rickety flights as if my legs were elastic. At last I'm in the courtyard. I shout again. They start to run, heading for the archway leading to the street. I must catch them before they head into the traffic. The younger girl trips on a loose brick and turns, her face flushed as a child's caught stealing a cookie. I help her up as the others escape into bedlam. "Two dollars," I say.

"Each?" She brushes her knees. They're scraped and bloody.

"Each." I command.

She searches her pockets. "I only have dong."

"Then give me the equivalent." I light the butt of an old cigarette I found in the courtyard to impress her with my importance.

"My friends," she pleads. "I must catch up—I—"

"I could call the police. I could have you jailed. You wouldn't like it. Our prisons are unpleasant, no television or air conditioning like in the States."

Tears form in her eyes. She is so lovely, like a forgotten goddess in a desecrated temple.

"If I give you the equivalent, I'll not have enough for a cab home."

"I'll ride you there on my bicycle."

"That's dangerous."

"I'll be cautious."

"One of my friends broke her arm on a bike."

"She must have been with an idiot." I stamp the butt beneath my feet.

"Give me the dong," I insist although I no longer feel like insisting. I would rather carry her upstairs, clean her wounds with antiseptic, dress the scrapes and bruises, bandage them with care and kiss them...

The Lonely Planet

THE MIST IS JUST LIFTING OFF Truc Bach Lake, the lake of the white bamboo. My father, Ba, and I have been shivering here since dawn, watching the vendors roll out straw mats and pillows, brew coffee, fry bananas and pineapple for the tourists who will soon arrive in big air-conditioned buses to visit the McCain Memorial. His Memorial is small, constructed of a yellowish stone. It nestles into the ground. Only McCain's head and torso are represented as if he'd lost the other parts of his body. You could easily miss the Memorial if the *Lonely Planet* did not tell you it was there.

John McCain is a great war hero to the Americans. He was shot down in his A4 aircraft over this very lake on October 26, 1967 by local citizens defending Yen Phu. I should hate him for bombing our women and children but somehow, I cannot. Both of his arms were broken in the fall and also one leg. Then he was dragged from the water and beaten before sent to the prison, Hoa Lo. Twice he tried to hang himself but was cut down by the guards and sent to solitary confinement for two years, iron shackles on his legs. They did not put shackles on his arms. There was no need.

Ba still hates McCain for what he did to our people; nevertheless, he is my personal hero. I hope he brings me good fortune today as my father and I have not had much luck of late. I must keep my feelings secret from Ba. He will be angry if I tell him how I worship John McCain and hope that when I grow up I will be able to withstand such torture. I have been to Hoa Lo and seen the cramped prison cells and the instruments of torture. It is difficult to believe that our soldiers would do such things. Ba says the Americans deserved even worse for what they did to us. But still, I cannot see that one crime deserves another. Hoa Lo is a luxury hotel now. Only one small portion has been preserved as a museum where visitors can imagine for themselves what McCain's life must have been like within those walls listening to Hanoi Hannah sing Vietnamese songs until his ears must have burst. No books, no mail, but then it would have been difficult to read beneath that single bulb burning in the ceiling. Prisoners tapped on walls to communicate. For five years he tapped on walls. No wonder he tried to hang himself.

Ba has a stack of *Lonely Planets* on the back of his bicycle. I rode here on the crossbar. Father is very strong. His leg muscles bulge; his arms can lift huge stacks of *Lonely Planets*. He can even lift the bicycle with me and the books still on it. That's how strong he is. I hope always he will be this strong. That he will never pass as my mother did at my birth. Ba tells me she was like a dancing star or a ray of pure sunshine. I sometimes look at the stars at night and see her dancing there. I call out for her to come and dance with me. "Ma come," I call, "please come. Hold me in your arms." I reach out hoping she will scoop me up into the flickering lights. But just as I feel her coming for me, she fades into the darkness. I am left alone like the *Planet* I am selling this morning. It is a guide book for tourists. But not a true guide book in that it is not true.

It is a knock-off of the real *Lonely Planet*. We can sell it at one third the price the tourists would pay in the States.

Father is skilled at knock-offs. Before we started selling this book we sold Gucci purses. "No one can tell the difference." Ba said. "They are just as happy with a fake, thinking they made a good bargain. It's the bargain they're after. That's what pleases them."

Ba gives me a rag, "Here," he says, "wipe down your hero so the tourists can read the inscription." If they cannot read it, they often turn away. The inscription is in Vietnamese, but I have learned some English in school, so I volunteer to translate the sign for a small price. Then I try to also sell them the guide book.

A hint of sun breaks through the palms now. Ba leaves the books with me and goes down to the lake with his string and stick to see if he can catch something for our lunch. I am always very hungry at lunch as we rode here early this morning from our village on the far side of Hanoi.

I settle myself on the stack of books pretending to read one. A tour bus stops. Opening its yellow doors, a crowd hurries down the steps, jostling each other in their rush to the Memorial. It is so small they could easily miss it. That's why I stand right next to it to make certain no one ignores my hero.

"What does it say?" They murmur to each other. "What does it—"

Politely I interrupt. "Let me help you." I hold out a copy of *Lonely Planet.* "If you buy this excellent guide book I will also read the inscription for you."

I am under grown for my age. I look like I am eight but I am really twelve. Since I do not threaten them by my size they stop and smile at me. "Yes, little boy, what does the inscription say?"

I return their smile making mine even brighter. "I will tell you when you buy this book. I sell it to you cheap."

In the distance I see other vendors approaching. If I do not hurry and make this sale, they will push in and steal it from me. They have done it many times before when I was shy and stuttered, so the tourists lost patience with me and turned to the other vendors who undercut my price. But I am older now and speak good.

"Shouldn't you be in school?" The lady asks. She seems tall as a young palm tree. Her bleached hair falls in fronds around her shoulders, but her skin is coarse and mottled as if she has slept in the sun since birth.

"I go to school this afternoon." In truth, I will only go to school today if I sell enough books to buy new tires for Ba's bike. His tires are ragged. "They will burst soon," he said as we rode here this morning. I love school and learning the English. I hope someday to go to America to practice the language.

The lady smiles. Her husband approaches. He's wearing a straw fisherman's hat that he must have bought in the market, blue flip-flops, white shorts and a red T-shirt with girls dancing on his chest. "From the look of that stack of books, I'd say we're your first customers today."

"Yes, Mister."

"Whatcha got there?"

"A very good guide book. You will need it in Hanoi. All our streets are mixed up. It has maps too, museums and restaurants, everything you want." I open the book to a clear map of Hanoi, careful not to reveal the blank pages in back or the pages where the print is so faint you can't read it.

"I think we need this, Doris." He unrolls some dong from his wallet. "This enough?"

"For that much I will read the inscription for you."

"This boy will read the inscription." Doris yells to the other members of their group who've been guessing at the words.

I have never had such a big audience before. My throat is suddenly dry, my knees shake, but I gather my courage. Climbing on top of my book stack to make myself heard, I recite the inscription which I've done so many times before I know it by heart.

When I finish, the crowd applauds, lining up to buy my books as if I were a national hero just like John McCain. My heart races with happiness. All my books will be sold. Ba will have new tires on his bike. He will pat my back; maybe even buy me an ice cream cone from the old woman at the corner. I can already taste the cold cream on my tongue. I feel it slip down my throat, sore from all that yelling. Then Ba will ride me to the school. I will boast to my friends about my good fortune. I will be their hero just like John McCain.

But as I calculate the dong I will soon have in hand, Doris tears the book's seal which I thought secure. The morning moisture must have weakened it. "Look, she says to her husband, "all these blank pages and the print… I can hardly read it."

My stomach trembles as if it were becoming sick with the diarrhea so common in my school.

Carefully, she closes the book and places it in my hands. "I'm sorry, little boy. I can't read this print. My eyes just aren't that good anymore."

I remove the dong from my pocket where it had been warm and safe and hold it out to her.

"It's all right," she rumples my hair, "you keep the money. But don't try to sell any more of your books. If someone should report you to the police, you'll be in trouble."

My heart sinks as McCain's must have when he was shot down over Truc Bach Lake. Sweat breaks out on my forehead at the thought of jail. Maybe the police would take me to Hoa Lo for my counterfeit books. Maybe they would jail me, shackle my legs so I could not escape. Maybe I would be there forever, never go to the school again or see Ba or lick the ice cream that he would buy for me.

The bus departs, churning dust, drowning the calls of the vendors. My *Lonely Planets* look lonelier than ever, like lost guides to a lake where the white bamboos have disappeared, taken over by bottles and cans, rotting oranges and banana peels. I squat beside my books trying to squash the tears that keep spurting from my eyes. Ba says I must not cry any more. I must learn to be a man. I rise beside my hero and prepare for the scolding my father will surely give me for not selling more books.

Ba comes up behind me and puts a hand on my shoulder. It's cold and smells faintly of the fish he must have in his basket. I see it trembling, drops of lake water shimmering on its gills. I smell it grilling over the fire Ba will make this noon from old newspapers, dry palm leaves and sticks...

But there is no fish in Ba's basket. We collect the books, load them on his bike, and tie them with his fishing string. I hop on the crossbar. "Come," he says. "We will try to take you to school."

Water

"*THUY,*" Tony called from below, "someone has come for you."

Tony was only twenty-two years old, yet he owned several massage parlors in Vietnam. The girls could not understand how he acquired such wealth at such a young age, as they can hardly support their children and husbands, that is, those who have husbands. They often brought their little ones to MEXICO MASSAGE. Tony did not mind as long as the babies were quiet, so we made sure we had the sleeping teddy bears to lull them while we played cards in silence until a customer arrived. Tony did not like to hear us laugh. He said it disturbed his concentration on the accounts.

It was now late in the afternoon. We have been waiting all day for someone to come. Most of our business was in the evening. Nevertheless, we must wait here all the day.

We waited in the big upstairs room with shaded windows overlooking Truc Bach Lane. The sweet smell of fried banana drifted up from the street below through our open windows. Sometimes, at the end of the night, the old vendor brought her leftovers up to us. They were heavy with grease by that hour. Bits of cinnamon burned their edges, but we had not eaten all day, so they were delicious.

Below our waiting room were showers and steam rooms. Most of our clients left their shoes in the hallway and stopped there first to purify themselves before the massage. Of course, there was an extra charge, but Tony would not allow us to serve anyone who had not stopped to bathe while we covered their cots with white sheets and pillows that we laundered that morning, beating them clean on the floors of the showers.

The small massage rooms lined the hallway so that many clients might be served at the very same time. Tony said that was good business. Tony knew about such things that we did not understand, having fled our villages to make our way in the big, noisy city of Hanoi.

Today, we dressed in white mini-skirts and tops. They were of a very smooth material that shone in the dark. I think it was called "satin." I liked to wear this outfit when I gave the massage, as it was easier to straddle the customer, to pull their arms and legs in many directions, relieving their stress.

Usually, I started on their heads, tugging strands of hair or massaging their scalps if the hair was thin or missing. Then I smoothed the wrinkles from their face with my thumb. It was like kneading bread dough. I pressed with thumb and finger, waited until the muscles relaxed before I took the head and swiveled it side to side as you would a doll's. At that moment the clients gasped as their tension released. And that was what I wished because my name meant "water." Water was a force of nature thus I have been blessed with this work, helping people feel as if water were flowing through them, sweet rivulets in all parts of their bodies.

Some clients wished only to have their heads massaged. If so, I spent much time on the scalp and hair line, tugging, smoothing, until the face became ten years younger.

Sometimes they wished only the feet. And so, with my own feet, I pressed the tension from theirs, released the eternal ache that caused them to stumble or hesitate crossing the traffic that the young navigated with such grace.

Today, an old woman arrived. She wanted a full body massage. She would not let me undress her, so I left the room for a moment, peeking in when she was lying on the table with the towel about her. "Where are you from?" I asked as I adjusted the towel that she placed over her nakedness.

"From the U.S.," she mumbled. I could see she did not wish to speak, only to sleep the half sleep of those who came to me, the dream state that was somewhere in the oblivion of all care.

She was a slim woman. I was grateful for that, as it made my work easier. Massaging through layers of fat was never simple, and sometimes the Americans have many layers.

"I am from Ho Chi Minh City," I said when I was certain I had made her comfortable. I was really from Hanoi, but I said I was from Ho Chi Minh City because that was a distance from Hanoi. People liked to ask about places that were distant. I made up stories about Ho Chi Minh City to please them, to make myself more mysterious. Hanoi was a place they saw every day, so it did not interest them. The recent floods made our streets almost impassable. They were filled with peels of apple, orange and banana. Mice and rats lay on their backs, their stomachs facing the sky, their little legs extended as if in prayer. Nothing could save them when the rains came as they do every year. But I am told this was the worst we have seen in thirty-seven years. Many people have died. Others were homeless, wandering the streets of Hanoi like ghosts. Even the dogs seemed to pity them.

I was grateful to live on the third floor of DC: 35 Chau Long-Truc Bach. The other girls returned to their villages as soon as the rains began. Tony barricaded the lower door with sand bags. No one was allowed to enter for the massage. No one dared to enter as the water rose higher. Traffic stalled, motor bikes were covered with plastic bags stolen from the market. We could not buy rice or oranges, noodles or vegetables. Downstairs, Tony and his mistresses ate what little they had. I was not one of his mistresses, so nothing was left for me except a spoonful of sticky rice and a saucer of tea. I grew so thin I hardly had the strength to climb down the dark stairway to receive my portion. Finally, when they remembered, they brought up a bowl of rice soup or green tea, chastising me for being so thin, telling me that if I did not grow stronger, they would leave me to the floods, let me float in the water with my legs apart to accompany the rats that glided so noiselessly past their shop, their "MEXICO MASSAGE."

"You will float to Mexico," they said, though none of them had ever been there. They did not even know where Mexico was. They got the name from a magazine. It was a beautiful magazine with photos of Mexican beaches and ladies lying on tables inside tents having their bodies massaged by pretty young women. Tony said I was beautiful enough to give the massage even though I might not be beautiful enough for anything else. And so, he gave me the job for which he did not pay. "Your clients will pay," he said. "They will tip if you treat them well."

Tony charged only 100,000 dong for the massage, less than anywhere else in Hanoi, so the tips were very small when they came at all. I was hoping this lady would leave me a big tip.

"Are you married?" I asked. I have been told this was the polite way to begin a conversation. "Yes," she breathed between closed lips.

I thought maybe she did not like to talk as I gave the massage, but I asked anyway. I said, "Do you have children?" She extended one finger.

"Boy or girl?"

"Boy." A smile crossed her face. I understood her joy, as boys were also preferred in Vietnam.

"How old are you?" I always asked the age of my clients as I massaged them. I could tell if they were lying by their skin, soft and supple or like the rind of a dragon fruit waiting to be sliced.

I never said they were lying. I tried to find something pleasant to say like, "You are very white. I am Viet, I am dark," as if their wrinkled white skin was better to have than my smooth brown one.

"Thank you," they whispered, probably thinking I was giving them a compliment.

This lady was very thin, like a withered doll, so I was careful when I massaged her arms. It was my custom to slap them, to bring blood to the surface, to wash away impurities. I slapped her gently, watching her loose skin jiggle like the flap beneath a turkey's neck.

"Are you okay?" I peered at her.

She opened her eyes. "Yes," she smiled from her daydream.

I raised the towel, the signal that she should turn on her stomach. She obliged with a sigh.

I kneaded her back. It was dry, so I asked if I might use some oil. It was Johnson's baby oil, made in America. I showed her the bottle. She laughed, so I knew I had pleased her.

I pummeled her buttocks. They were large for such a small person, an indication that she spent too much time sitting, and so they spread. She left on her panties, so I pulled them down to get at the soft flesh beneath, oiled and pounded it to the desired firmness. But the desired firmness did not occur no matter how much I pounded, so I descended to her legs, long and thin like the loaves of French bread they sold in the market. Her toes were brittle as the crusts, her thighs spongy as the interior.

I helped her to sit up. By this time, she was not embarrassed to reveal her small, child-like breasts, which I had carefully avoided. Her back was spotted as a banana too long in the sun. I tried to bleach it with my special potion but the spots would not fade no matter how much I smoothed them.

"You are very beautiful," I said as I stared at the clock to make the last minutes pass quickly. I wished to meet Anh. I heard his motorbike pull onto the curb below where the lady sat selling papaya until the police rounded the corner. Then she ran inside our shop before they caught her selling without a license.

Murmuring other compliments, I helped my client to dress. She wore very few garments for one so old, but they said that was the way in America.

I waited for her tip, hoping it would be a large one as I worked very hard to make her feel like water. She showed me 100,000 dong. I motioned, yes, that was for me and tried to take it from her hand. But she pointed below where Tony waited. I followed her down the stone steps, helped her to slip on the wedged sandals she had left on the staircase.

Tony was dressed today in a black suit and yellow shirt. He smelled of coconut oil. On his purple tie a palm tree waved. A Mexican girl grinned beneath his diamond stick pin. His alligator shoes shone as he approached the cash register.

My client showed him the bill, 100,000 VND as he advertised in big electric letters so no one could miss them even in the dark. She presented a 10,000 dong tip for me. For this I might buy two loaves of French bread and some bananas. I tried to smile.

Tony looked at me and hesitated. She removed our white calling card from her purse, which read in black letters, MEXICO MASSAGE, 100,000 VND. Tony glanced at my face again. I hoped he would beg something more for me, but he accepted her dong, creased it between his long nails that I filed and painted with colorless lacquer on days when we had no customers.

"Okay?" she said.

"Okay—okay," he waved, ignoring me.

A motorbike rumbled outside, an angry roar that encouraged me. "I am leaving," I told Tony as he closed the register.

"You are what?"

"I am leaving," I repeated. His face clouded as if another storm were brewing over Truc Bach Lake, another disaster.

"Where will you go?" he said clicking his nails on the counter. "For girls like you, there is nothing."

I hurried to the door, my 10,000 dong gripped in my fist. Anh will drive me around the lake, I thought, my arms hugging his waist. We will buy French bread and bananas, savor them on a bench as we drink in the moon and kiss the sun awake.

I rushed outside to tell him I was free from MEXICO MASSAGE, free to ride to Ho Chi Minh City, free to—

"Where is he?" I called to the boys repairing motor-bikes at the curb.

"Where is who?" They kept on with their work, wiping the sweat that oozed from their eyes, trickled down their necks onto their bright T-shirts.

"The one who always comes for me."

"We did not see him."

"You must have. I heard his bike. It has a special roar."

"For you, maybe," they laughed. "For us, they are all the same."

The Silk Emporium

THE SIGN ON MY SHOP BLINKS SILK EMPORIUM in large electric letters. You can't miss the sign even when the rain blinds you. Next door there is also a silk shop. In fact, there are many silk shops in Old Town. That's why I chose to name mine SILK EMPORIUM. In these difficult times, one must employ every advantage to get ahead. It's not as if there were no other merchants in Hanoi anxious to close my doors in order to keep theirs open. Oh, we pretend we're not rivals. Each morning, when we sweep the sidewalk in front, we greet each other over our bamboo brooms as if we were one family truly concerned with each other's health and well-being. In reality, we wish each other nothing but illness and bad fortune so that we might prosper.

I've never confessed this before. Perhaps I never believed this, allowing myself to be deceived by small courtesies, such as the time I had a sick stomach and Li left a bowl of noodle soup on my doorstep. When I didn't come down from my rooms above to taste the soup, her daughter left a cup of herb tea on my step, knocking thrice to make certain I heard and would sip the tea while it was hot. I pretended not to hear the knocks only drinking the tea after I heard her sandals slap against the light rain that had begun to fall as it does many afternoons in Hanoi. That way I didn't have to thank her, could pretend a cat had lapped the tea and thus the empty cup. But Li would not give up continuing to annoy me with her solicitude as if I were some orphan that needed caring.

Indeed, she was right in that regard, my parents having left me with the Sisters of Mercy when I was an infant. They had eleven other children and couldn't afford another spoonful of rice for the twelfth.

I know that if I accept anything from Li, I must return the favor. That's our custom. I don't wish to dwindle my limited resources in that kind of exchange, each one seeing how she could best the other, give a less expensive gift for one more costly.

I'm standing in my doorway now watching the tourists flee for shelter before the next cloudburst. It's nearing five. Most of them will hail a rickshaw to drive them back to their hotels. How I would love to be driven back to a hotel rather than the dark rooms above my shop that stink from the dust of the streets, the bird droppings littering my window sill, the greasy smell of frying fish. I've never been in a hotel and maybe never will be. It's my wish that on my honeymoon my husband will take me to a grand hotel. But since I have no hope for a husband as I'm beyond the age of hoping, I must abandon that wish as I have so many others.

The rain is heavier now. Little puddles form where the dogs have slept. The peanut seller covers his wagon and moves on, the fish monger sits beneath his cart, the mango lady tries to hover in my doorway, but I shush her off, afraid the tourists won't enter if she blocks their way. She curses me and spits on my step. I pretend to ignore her but inside I shudder, my stomach churning as if it would escape her wrath.

My electric sign grows dim, finally goes dark as thunder strikes. I hurry into the rain with my umbrella, hoping to lure any last tourist into my shop. Soon I see them, this fat girl and a thin grayish woman who must be her mother. The girl's hair is bright as an overripe orange, her skin freckled as the spotted sheets on my neighbor's line. Her mother frowns, grasping the girl's arm as they dodge the rain drops. I rush toward them, offering my umbrella, inviting them into the Emporium.

"We're wet." The mother wipes drips from the girl's forehead.

"It does not matter. Here, stand beneath the fan to dry yourselves."

I fetch a rag and kneel to wipe their feet.

"We can do that," the mother protests.

"It's my pleasure," I say, thinking now that they're inside my shop with the rain pounding my roof they will surely buy something even if it's just a silk umbrella to send them on their way.

"Please sit and have some tea to refresh you."

"Oh no, we couldn't. We're late getting back to the hotel as it is."

The daughter says nothing. She's already pawing the garments, shaking her wet hair on my new straw mats as she admires herself in the mirror.

"Don't make a mess," the mother barks, joining her daughter at the dress rack.

"These fabrics are delicate," I tell them. "Some have Paris labels." I'd sewn the labels in carefully after I'd copied the designs from *ELLE*. I love the texture of silk, its sensuous surface, the way it clings to the breasts and hips of a small, slender girl such as I once was.

"They're exquisite." The mother unrolls a bolt of silk the shade of cinnamon while her daughter tries on everything that doesn't fit.

"Be careful, dear, you could burst the seams."

"Would that be a problem?" she says to me as she tries to zip some indigo trousers over her bulging stomach.

"Of course not. We'd just sew them up again."

"This is a beautiful bolt of pink silk." The mother traces her long manicured nails over the shiny fabric. "Maybe she could make something for you."

The girl smiles tossing the trousers on the floor as she grabs a red sheath from a hanger and starts to drag it over her head. "Help me, Mom, it's stuck."

"One moment, I'll see if I have a larger size in back."

The girl doesn't answer as she's still stuck inside the dress. "Mom," she whines, "I can't pull it down."

"Pull it up then," the mother mumbles, busy trying on jackets.

In back I rummage through the storeroom, hoping I'll find a larger size, but there's nothing larger, only smaller as would fit an American twelve-year-old. I must find something, I think. They will not leave my shop without a purchase.

Finally, I spot a bolt of white silk secluded on a high shelf. I climb the ladder and carry it down on my shoulder, sweat dripping down my neck, staining my favorite blouse, pale yellow with a lotus blossom trim. The blouse was a present from the Sisters of Mercy who still remember my birthdays even though it's many years since I have seen them.

Carefully I blow dust from the bolt of white silk. It's bridal white, pure and hopeful. I'd saved it for the wedding I never had and never will. So why not sell it now, why not get some profit from a dream that proved to be worthless. It's a heavy roll. I squat to wedge it through the doorway hoping my sweat doesn't stain it and ruin the sale.

The girl has managed to extricate herself from the dress and thrown it over a lopsided stool in the corner. Her mother is fitting her scrawny body into a mauve silk jacket much too large for her.

"Can you take it in?" she asks as I carefully roll the white silk to her feet, pushing my bangs from my forehead, where sweat has plastered them.

"My pleasure." I get some pins from my sewing machine and begin to pinch the jacket. But it's no use.

The woman is a stick, so it hangs limply. "Perhaps we can find something else. This white silk would complement your hair."

"I'm thinking of changing the color, dyeing it black while I'm in Vietnam. Hairdressers are so much cheaper here than in the States."

"Your hair is lovely as it is."

I unroll the silk and hold it against her. "See, white is just the color for you. I've been to the fashion schools in Paris. I know such things." In truth, I've never been outside Hanoi. But the silk is white and so is the lie and thus can be forgiven.

"Really?"

"Why would I tell you a falsehood? It might keep me from entering the gates of heaven when I pass."

"You're religious?"

"Of course, the afterlife is to be cherished. It makes the indignities of this one bearable."

"I never thought of it that way, since I find this life perfectly enjoyable."

"We better go, Mom. The kids are waiting. If I'm late, they'll go for beer without me."

"I don't want you going for beer. It'll bloat your stomach."

"Well I'm going anyway." She starts to leave.

"You're not going anywhere without me."

"Who says?" And she's out the door.

"Carolla, come back here."

But it's no use. The girl has disappeared into the storm.

"Wait," I call after them. "I have an umbrella for you. It's a fine silk. It can be used rain or shine."

But the woman doesn't hear. She hails a cab which doesn't stop. I plod after her, two umbrellas beneath my arm. "Here," I yell. "Take these. I'll sell them to you cheap."

She ignores me, boarding a trishaw hooded with plastic. Her daughter suddenly emerges from a shop down the street and climbs in beside her.

"Here," I call again shaking the umbrellas. "These will protect you."

But they've already rounded the corner. I open an umbrella and trudge back to my shop in time to see the leaks form in my ceiling. I set out pots to catch the drips as I have every year. Lifting the bolt of white silk from the floor, I carry it back to the storeroom and set it on the shelf beside the other unsold bolts of fabric. I slump there, wondering how I can pay the rent, which is higher every year, how I can buy enough rice before the monsoon sets in, how I can pay someone to fix the leaks, how I can …

Suddenly I hear three knocks. I descend my ladder and hurry to the door, thinking it might be a tourist attracted by my sign, which has begun to blink again. I open the door. Li hovers there, a cup of herb tea in hand.

"I—I couldn't help noticing… I—I just thought you might need …"

"Don't stand there in the rain, Li. Come in, come in … We'll sip tea together …"

Snow

I AM CALLED SNOW because snow was falling in Jinan the day I was born. "It was piled high in the streets," my mother said, "like so many small Buddha Mountains. It was beautiful to see as you were beautiful that special day. Your father wanted a boy, of course, but secretly I wanted a girl. I have never told him that, never told him how happy I was that you, my Snow, were given to me."

I have lived in Jinan all my life. But now that my mother has gone, I long to leave it, its sky, like a plate of porridge with a dollop of butter where the sun should be. I have read there are cities in the world where the streets are clean and the sun shines bright all the day. How I long for such warmth.

I am here in the Shandong University clinic because of an infection. I am not certain how I got this infection but it has caused me much pain. Today is the third day I am coming here to recover from this illness. The doctor has given me a prescription which is in the vial above me. It drips through a long plastic snake into my hand. The nurse inserted a needle to draw blood. Now, through that incision, the healing potion flows.

In the bed next to me is an Accounting student. She is in her second year. Orange—that is her favorite color, so that is how she calls herself—is very optimistic about her future. "I want to be an international CPA," she giggles behind her palm, her black hair swishing like the tail on a new pony.

I wish her well as she turns from me to sleep. I wish everyone well, that is my habit of late. Of course, it wasn't always that way. At one time I was jealous of all who were under thirty, who sought bright futures. But now I see how foolish that was. They could no more help desiring brightness than I could help resigning myself to the darkness which I fear might become my fate.

On the other side of my cot, next to the rain streaked window, lies an American student who coughs in spasms. She does not know what is wrong with her only that she, like many people in Jinan, cannot stop coughing. The doctors X-rayed her lungs to see if she has the dreaded TB, but fortunately, the result is negative.

"I waited in line with those freshmen taking their military training," she complains. "I couldn't believe they were still using equipment like that. I thought China was well, like, a—a—modern country. I mean, like they just had the Olympics and all, ya know."

It is difficult for me to answer but I try my best to help her understand that my country is still developing.

"We are trying to become modern," I say. "But it is difficult when there are over a billion people even though we are limited to one child per family. If it's a girl you can try again in six years, but that rule only applies to the countryside."

"Bummer," she says as she inspects the flaking walls of this clinic that is especially for teachers, students, and their families.

The old sweeper enters. He is as bent as his broom. A large surgical bandage covers his forehead. I can only imagine what terrible wound it conceals. He sweeps some debris from the floor and empties it into the trash container. As he starts to carry the trash away, the American points to the lights. She knows no Chinese so is reduced, like a child, to pointing and waving. He obliges with a bow, turning on the ceiling fluorescent, the others do not work.

The girl reaches for the Call button to tell the nurse that her medication bottle is nearly empty. But the Call button does not work either.

I get up from my bed and lift my vial from its cradle. Holding it above me, I walk the grimy corridor to the nurses' station. I wait my turn to speak as she is busy filling other prescriptions. Her blue smock is frayed around the edges. Safety pins hold up her torn pockets, but her eyes are gentle behind her surgical mask. She follows me back to the bed where the American waits, adjusting her lumpy pillow, smoothing her soiled sheets which have not been changed between patients.

The nurse removes her empty vial and returns with a full one, checking to see that it flows correctly into the girl's hand, advising her not to disturb the needle.

"What'd she say?" the girl asks.

"She told you to keep your hand still," I answer with pleasure, as I am a teacher of English at Shandong University.

"What'd you say?" the girl asks again, looking confused.

I repeat what I'd said. She frowns. Again, I tell her but she seems dense and does not understand me even though I speak slowly for her benefit.

"Oh," she sighs. I think she finally understands, as she lies very still as if she were dead. I wonder what would happen if she did die. How would they transport her back to America? I envision her in a cart pulled through the streets of Jinan by men stinking of sweat, their muscles tight and sore with exhaustion. Behind her cars blow their horns while drivers talk on cell phones. We know it is dangerous to talk on cell phones while driving but no one pays attention to such warnings. They think it is cool to be seen talking on a cell phone. That is why we have so many accidents, because no one pays attention.

It was that way coming here this morning. I tried to cross between cars and bicycles. Many, many bicycles but also the cars have increased, never slowing, blowing their horns instead to frighten me. The guards at the North gate tried to control them but they just blew louder. I was almost struck as I crossed but swerved just in time, landing on a cart full of oranges, bananas, and kiwi. The vendor tried to charge me for squashing his fruit, but a policeman chased him off and helped me to the clinic. As it had rained the night before, the streets were slick so we jumped puddles to the crowded courtyard where the mob of freshmen in khaki uniforms waited at the entrance for eye exams. The exams were necessary to be eligible for the weeks of military training. Holding a paper over one eye, they read with the other, looking pleased if they passed the test.

I placed a mask over my mouth to dispel the noxious odor of the toilet as I rushed to the cashier's window before the freshmen would finish their exams and crowd me out. I deposited the necessary yuan before I could see the doctor. Placing the receipt in my pocket, I climbed to the second floor and waited outside the doctor's office. There were three physicians so I chose the one where the line was shortest, only two families ahead of me waiting in the dingy hallway.

Finally, the doctor signaled me. Her hair fell in gray wisps over her surgical mask. Her sallow face was wrinkled and dry as the skin of a forgotten lemon. She listened to my heart through the stethoscope hanging about her neck. Her breath smelled of onion and garlic as she wrote a prescription. I brought the prescription downstairs to another window and waited once more, then paid my yuan and proceeded to the nurses' station. After my blood was drawn, I was given the medication that is flowing into my hand.

"I would like to go to your country," I tell the American to make conversation between her coughs. She looks at me with eyes the shade of blue on an emperor's porcelain. Her hair is spiked and blonde as if she has recently visited a salon where they color it to order.

"Why?" she smiles as if my reference to her country delights her. "I've always wanted to come to China. It's so, like, well, different. That's why I'm here with these kids from California. But I've, like, spent most of my time at this clinic." She coughs again.

"I am sorry."

"Oh, it's okay. I guess it's to be expected, all this pollution and stuff. But you, you must be used to it."

"We never get used to it. It is simply our way of life. My husband is lucky. He travels frequently selling sports equipment for American companies with outlets in China. In fact, he is away right now." I feel myself wince as the pain comes again.

"Is it this thick in all of China?" The girl coughs and reaches for her water bottle.

"No, there are places in the mountains or near the beaches that I am told are clean because there are no cars or factories. Maybe someday I will be lucky enough to visit them."

"How come you're here? I mean, you look pretty healthy and all." She gazes at me with those wide eyes, the double creases on her lids lending them a pop star's splendor.

I watch the potion slowly drip into our hands. The fluid contains glucose, some sodium and vitamin C to make our bodies strong enough to recover without medication. "I—I have an infection." I hesitate as the pain surges upwards.

"What kind?" I mean, it's okay if you don't want to say.

It is difficult to tell her, like revealing a secret between my husband and myself. When I told my husband, I had a vaginal infection he did not believe me. "How did you get it?" he shouted between bursts of shower water.

He liked to wash his hair every morning, smooth it with pomades so that it glistened in the lamp light. We have a modern apartment, on the seventh floor of a walkup on the west side of Jinan. At one time there was talk of installing an elevator but that never happened. The building has only been erected four years but already the exterior is crumbling, the pipes in the bathroom rusting, the electricity often out.

On the Sunday I told him of my infection, he came from the shower in his slippers, a towel around his hips. His buttocks were slender, almost as thin as a boy's. I loved his thighs, the genitals curved deeply between them, muscles strong and supple. He turned on the television. We have a large television, almost the length of the wall. We loved to watch it, reclining on the soft beige couch that curved the corners of our apartment. That morning a soccer match was playing. "How did you get the infection?" he repeated as he dried himself with the towel. It had the imprint of the last hotel he had visited.

I looked at him and rolled more dough for the dumplings I always prepared for Sunday breakfast. I filled one with the pork and onion mixture I had prepared earlier that morning before my husband rose.

"I am hungry." he yawned. "Will they be ready soon?"

"The water is almost to boil. I will steam them shortly."

"I hope so. I have to leave again."

"But it is Sunday. Do you have business even today?"

"I am ambitious. I always have business." He went into the bedroom to dress while I steamed the dumplings. Drops of perspiration ran down my face. He came from the bedroom in his sports outfit and sat at the table tying his Adidas. He smelled of his favorite French cologne.

"I thought you had business."

"I am meeting some friends first for soccer."

"Will you return for lunch? I could prepare orange chicken and beef in crab oil."

"I do not think I will be back this afternoon. I might return this evening depending on how things go."

"Would you like me to wait dinner for you?"

"If you like, but do not depend on my arrival."

I set the plate of dumplings on the table. They smelled sweet. I had added some bean curd to the pork. He skewered one on his chopstick and waved it to cool the dough before he bit in. "Good," he said between mouthfuls.

I watched him eat, happy that he found my dump-lings to his liking. I did not want to bring up the subject of the infection again as it seemed to make him angry. I collected his plate when he finished, washed it, and set it on the drain to dry.

"Are you not eating?" He asked.

"Later perhaps. I am not hungry now."

"That is too bad. Your dumplings are better when they are hot."

"I can boil more water, reheat them."

"Your infection," he belched as he left the table, "how did you get it?" He stared at me as he pulled his baseball cap low over his deep-set eyes that had just begun to wrinkle at the corners.

"I do not know," I whispered.

"I might surprise you this evening, come home a bit early. But don't wait up." He slammed the door behind him. I heard his key turn in the lock, which meant he expected me to remain at home waiting his return. I went to the kitchen and retrieved a half-eaten dumpling. It was cold. I tried to swallow it anyway but it caught in my throat.

For several moments I did not speak as I dwelled on that memory. Finally, my voice returns although it does not sound like my voice but as if someone else were speaking. "The doctor said it is a vaginal infection but I am hoping he is wrong. I would like to have a child, a boy, it would please my husband."

"What would you name him?"

"Yuan. Money is very important to my husband. We would name him after my husband's deepest desire."

The girl laughs, "Yeah, that's the big item in my country too. I thought it might be different here. In fact, I was hoping, like, maybe I could find another place somewhere that maybe, like, ya know, all that stuff wasn't so important. Know what I mean?"

"I think I do, but I have never found one. Such places are only in my dreams now..."

We watch the final drops of fluid flow into our veins. Our vials are empty.

Stairway To Heaven

EVERY MORNING while it's still dark, I ascend the Stairway to Heaven hoping to arrive with the sun at the mountain home of the God, Tai Shan, the most powerful god in all China. Rain fell in the night so the 7,000 steps are slippery. I climb carefully; one fall on the jagged bricks could finish my ascent, leaving me bloody and broken with no human to give me aid. At this early hour vendors are still asleep, shops and temples closed. I'm a lone pilgrim. But I must somehow make the ascent once again even though my cough has gotten worse. I frequently stop to clear my lungs, the green phlegm in my chest spattering the stairway. But others have done the same. Dried blood stains the bricks black. Patterns of yesterday's mucus swirl designs in the corners of the bricks that the night rain failed to wash clean. Oh, Bixia Yuanjin, Goddess of the Dawn, I pray, heal me, protect my ascent as you have all the women who came before me, even those with bound feet, stumbling and crawling their way to the top.

But my prayers only induce more phlegm. I stop to breathe deeply, lean on my walking stick, clear my lungs and continue. Even though it's cold and I'm wrapped well in my padded jacket and thick pants, I've begun to sweat. It's not normal perspiration, a result of being overdressed, it's a kind of clamminess that concerns me, as if some inner defect were surfacing, warning me of a trauma that could occur if I insist on this daily climb. But I must persist. It's my livelihood, for I'm the protector of the Goddess Bixia. I must sit in the Temple of the Purple Dawn as the sun rises until it sets when I descend the holy mountain and take the bus to my village. I'd like some day to ride the cable car half way, to fly through the clouds instead of plodding my way on foot. But I can't afford the ride; all my earnings must support my old husband who's too ill to work and my unmarried daughter who cares for him while I protect the Goddess.

Suddenly I hear shouts from below echoing through the mist, a girl's scream, then laughter, much laughter. I sense their approach, but the gloom is so heavy I see only their silhouettes. Melding into the darkness, I step aside for them to pass. I become part of the drizzle or simply a cypress growing along the path, my branches twisted in the wind that howls above.

They draw closer, their bodies young and vibrant as if no wind had ever touched them, or any stroke of misfortune. They leap up the steps stretching their long legs like flamingoes in the lake below. One girl is blonde as the moon, thin as a sapling. She wears jeans cut off just below her groin and a thin halter that barely conceals her nubile breasts. I must tell her there are great-coats for sale at the summit. She might fall ill in such flimsy attire. But she seems oblivious of the chill. Her boyfriend wraps his arms about her. He's taller than she, six feet or more, a young tattooed giant with long hair, blonde as hers, only tied in a ponytail beneath his baseball cap. They stand for several minutes immersed in each other before the rest of their group arrives, smoking and shouting, sipping cans of beer, more bulge from their backpacks. Shandong University emblazons their T-shirts. I wish to silence them, send them back to their university to learn reverence for the Five Sacred Mountains, study the legends of Pang Gu, the first ruler of the universe whose head became the Eastern Mountain, his chest the Central, his left arm the Southern, his right arm the Northern and his feet the Western. Thus, Mount Tai became the head of the Five Sacred Mountains. He's not to be trod lightly, climbed without awareness of his power. Who knows what ills might befall them if they ignore him.

The students disappear into the fog. Their voices recede like the wails of ghosts that are believed to inhabit the caves of this mountain, the craggy recesses where hermits abide in prayer. Some are said to be 400 years old or more, surviving on herbs that grow along these slopes, drinking from streams that rush the mountain sides.

I emerge from my hiding place. A hint of light leaks through the darkness, a shimmer of rain rustles the trees. Shivering inside my jacket, I wish myself at the top, but I've hundreds of feet left to climb. A spattering of blood when I cough, its rosy hue flowers the Stairway to Heaven. I give my blood to the Sacred Mountain. There's nothing more I can give to insure long life, the 100 years promised those who climb to the top. But do I really wish my life to be much longer? It must be, I think, yes it must. What will my husband do if I'm gone or my daughter? They wait for me to return each night, my pockets crammed with the steamed bread I buy before I board the bus. My husband relishes the bread because he's lost all his teeth from the illness. The bread can be gummed to a pulp before he swallows with a cup of green tea to wash it down. His hand trembles as he traces the blue design on the cup, a wedding gift from his mother. I place my hand over his to help the cup to his lips. He's so frail, growing weaker each day. But the thought of his passing sends a cold wind through me. The warmth of my life would be gone, the fire extinguished. My daughter and I would live like robots repeating the routines of the day with no heart behind it. Yes, I must live to be 100 only if he is by my side.

In the distance, a rooster crows, chickens cluck, shutters swing back on the pagodas scattered along the way. Here and there a monk emerges from the forest, begging bowl in hand. I bow my head in reverence but have nothing to give, so he turns away.

I can just see the summit now, a few more steps and I'm there. A glint of sun burnishes the clouds. I must hurry or the sun will rise without me, leave Bixia unprotected, open to molesters, those who deface her temple, steal tributes left by pilgrims, chocolate pudding boxes, bottles of water, apples and oranges or scatterings of yuan in hopes Bixia will grant their prayers, their wish to conceive. Goddess of the Dawn, she attends the birth of each new day from her home high in the clouds. Goddess of Childbirth, she oversees the arrival of children, fixing their destiny and bringing good fortune. Long ago, she granted my wish to conceive, gave me a beautiful daughter for which I'm grateful. She's brought me nothing but joy, her face like the sun every morning, her voice high as a mountain flute, her step light as a fairy's.

I rush to unlock the temple, swing back the heavy door. Bixia glows in the dim light. I kowtow before her, dust the altar with the feathers of ducks; sweep the floor with my bamboo broom. And then, when all is ready, I drag my wooden box outside into the warming air and wait for the sun to rise.

Those who live in the village at the summit are already busy. The aroma of Jian Bing drifts from the food stalls. I long for some egg spread thick with soy sauce, wrapped around a fresh green onion. When the lunch hour arrives, I promise myself, I will buy one from my favorite vendor, the woman with one blind eye. Her onions are always fatter, easier to crunch between my teeth, the bite of it filling my mouth for hours. Even asleep, I still taste it.

Gradually the staircase crowds with tourists. Some have taken the cable car part way, the bus before that. Others have walked, their faces grim with effort. They search for the WC. It's hidden behind some trees as if it were ashamed of the filth. It's rarely cleaned, so the air is foul. Tourists hurry from it pressing a mask to their faces. I for one prefer the bushes. At least the air is fresh there. And there is no waiting.

Bixia glows behind me. I cherish the sweetness on her face, its benevolence. A tourist approaches, the red band of long life and prosperity wrapped around her graying head. She smiles at me. "Is it true," she whispers, "that Bixia will help me conceive? I've been to fertility clinics at home but none has helped. Next year I'll be forty-one. My time will soon be past."

She extends her hand. I warm her cold fingers. "It's true," I murmur. "Bixia has that power. You must believe in her with all your heart."

She presses some yuan into my hand before she slips inside the temple. I secrete them inside my egg pocket. I'll count them later, hoping they'll purchase enough eggs for the evening meal with my family.

The morning passes into afternoon, and still, the mist has not lifted. I drift into sleep on my box, not the heavy sleep of night but a twilight rest through which I can still discern the visitors to Bixia, hear their footsteps, their laughter as they notice my head nod on my chest. The climb has exhausted me. Someday, I fear I'll collapse on those steps and have to be carried down by boys young enough to be my grandchildren. They'll brush the matted hair from my face; mop the sweat from my brow. "Don't worry, Auntie," they'll say, "trust us. We've taken CPR at school. We have our certificates."

I'll close my eyes with relief, and allow myself to be cared for by children, wishing those boys were my daughter's, that I would go home with them to my village. They would sing along the way as the bus rocked and rolled on the rutted road. "Grandma," they'd whisper as they snuggled next to me, "we're almost there."

When I open my eyes, the sun is setting. Reentering the temple, I make certain no joss sticks still burn. I save the yuan scattered on the altar for the monk who'll collect it tomorrow. I kowtow to Bixia before I padlock the door. Her face is radiant in the evening light as if she's conceived once again and anticipates the birth of many children.

In the distance, the shouts of students descending echo through the cypress. Stooping, I retrieve the empty beer cans they've discarded and drop them into my knapsack. I'll trade them for yuan when I reach the bottom. It will be enough to buy some steamed bread along with the eggs and maybe a fat green onion or two. We'll have Jian Bing tonight for dinner thick with soy sauce. Saliva fills my mouth. I already taste the onion. I hope it lasts the night.

The Palace of
Peace and Harmony

I CALL MYSELF MARK. It's easy on the tongue, a single syllable, nothing much to remember. And that's what I expect from the tourists, that they'll not remember me, not recall the infinite patience I've employed to help them pronounce the names of our gods, repeating them again and again. Still, I never give the slightest indication that they might be stupid, the smallest hint that they left their brains at home.

I tell them I'm a scholar of Lama Buddhism and Confucius, that I'm studying for a degree in International Relations. I've repeated this so many times I've come to believe it myself. In truth, it's my dearest wish, a dream that will never come true. If I'd been born into a different family, instead of the son of some woman I do not remember... She abandoned me in the trash outside this very temple, this Palace of Peace and Harmony. I was retrieved by the monks who raised me as well as they could. Spending most of their day in prayer, they left me with the cleaning woman, Ahn, who did her best to see that I didn't get into mischief.

I hear the monks now. As a child their chanting lulled me to sleep in the tiny arms of Ahn. She was not much bigger than I as her feet had been bound so that her legs never developed properly. Her trunk remained stunted like that of a tree the rain had never watered. She was from the north, her dialect different from that of the monks. She was kind in her way but always tired as the temple was large with many courtyards and corridors to sweep and idols to shine to such brilliance that the passerby was forced to kowtow before them, to drop some yuan in their baskets, to light many joss sticks in hopes the god would grant their prayers. I often helped her clean, picking up cigarette butts that she pocketed, tearing them apart later, rolling fresh cigarettes from the bits I collected. She also pocketed fruit left on altars before the monks found them. She was a crafty soul. It was from her I learned my trade of modest deception in order to survive the rigors of Beijing.

At this moment a crowd is forming outside waiting for the ceremony to begin. It occurs only twice a lunar month. I hear the drums now, the horns, the clang of cymbals, the chanting. It will continue for two hours. For two hours I'll watch the crowd, circulate among the strangers who seem intoxicated by the incense, the flowers, the kneeling monks resembling flamingoes at rest, heads bowed in supplication.

It's cold in Beijing this morning. Rain fell last night bathing the temple with mist. The gutters are full, the worn steps slick. I tread them with caution. They've been trod since 1694 when the temple was built to be the residence of the Quing Dynasty's Prince Yong. After Yong's ascension to the throne in 1722 half of the building was converted into a lamasery. The other half remained an imperial palace. Yong's successor gave the temple imperial status by having its turquoise tiles replaced with yellow ones that reflect the sun when it chooses to shine through the gray pall that envelopes this city. Somehow it survived the Cultural Revolution to be reopened in 1981 as the national center of Lama Administration and thus a star tourist attraction.

I follow the tourists through the courtyards making myself inconspicuous by dressing in black with a sweater the color of this dull morning beneath my jacket. I stand in the shadow of the great hall observing the kneeling monks, kneeling myself at times on the small pillows placed behind them by the faithful who chant with the monks, hypnotized by their voices, by the gong and cymbal. I chant also as I did in my childhood, inhaling the sweet incense, almost forgetting my purpose. The growling in my stomach reminds me that I've not eaten since yesterday's lunch and must somehow procure lunch today, must charm some visitors into inviting me to join them.

A woman dressed in a bright pink windbreaker leans against the temple wall. Her hair is as gray as my

sweater. Her husband's is as white as the candles deco-
rating the altar. Their attention is rapt to the ceremony.
I'll wait, I think, for the break in prayers to address
them. It would be foolish to disturb them now and lose
any chance of joining them for lunch.

"Are you from California?" I say when an intermission
finally arrives. The woman smiles. "How did you know?"

"You're wearing a jacket the color of flamingoes."

"Really?"

"Yes, it's so cheerful. All of our California guests
seem happy."

"Must be the sunshine," she laughs.

I admire her even white teeth so different from my
own, mottled by incessant smoking. I've tried to give
up the habit I inherited from Ahn but as they say, old
habits die hard. Besides, smoking is a national pastime
in China. Smelling tobacco intoxicates me. I've even
inherited her habit of rescuing butts and rolling my
own. I've been doing this since I was twelve.

"How did you hear about this celebration?" I
inquire with all the finesse I can muster.

"Our concierge, she told us," the husband chimes in
eagerly. He's a thin man, wiry as a weasel, a hint of frugality.

"You're at the Hilton?" I ask thinking the better the
hotel, the better the lunch.

"No, we're stayin' at the Sun Palace. The price is right."

A sense of disappointment envelopes me. But
still, lunch is lunch. At this moment I'd eat a rat if it
were offered.

"Please excuse me, I forgot to introduce myself. My name is Mark. I'm a student at the university studying for my Master's in International Relations."

"How impressive." She zips her jacket against the cold as if she were about to depart.

I must keep them here until lunch time, I think, so I say, "I'm also studying Buddhism. That's why I spend so much time here."

"All right." The weasel rubs his hands together. It's obvious he's not used to cold weather.

"May I escort you through the rest of the grounds? You could easily get lost in the maze." I button my jacket hoping to muffle the growling in my gut.

"I'd love it." She seems somewhat confused. "At this moment I'm not certain we'd ever find our way out."

"Sure we would, honey." He pats her shoulder. "I've a damned good sense of direction, remember? Always have had."

"Don't discount your GPS," she murmurs.

"Listen, babe, even before I bought Global Positioning my sense of direction was right on."

"I'm not saying a word." She shifts her purse to the opposite shoulder as if his remarks add to her discomfort.

"There are five main halls," I interject lest a major argument erupt and they flee the temple leaving me lunch-less. "Each one will enlighten us further, help us to understand this ancient religion. You'll return to California imbued with new knowledge. Maybe you'll even lead tours here in the future. Would you like that?"

The woman beams with the vision of her importance while the weasel frowns at the burden of more responsibility. I wonder if he likes fish for lunch, a large carp or a sweet piece of shark. "I take you first to the Hall of Harmony and Peace." I smile to soothe any jagged nerves that still remain. They're stunned into silence by the bronze Buddhas of the Three Ages.

Next, we visit the Hall of Everlasting Protection where the healing Buddha stands. I often come here when I have the flu or some other respiratory infection that's the bane of living in Beijing, one of the most polluted cities in China, perhaps in all the world. I'd love to leave here, travel the perimeters of the earth, savor the cuisine of every country. But for now, I must settle for lunch and hope it's a good one.

I figure the Hall of the Wheel of Law will appeal to the weasel. It contains a carving made of red sandalwood with statues of the arhats made from five different precious metals, gold, silver, copper, iron and tin. The weasel's eyes glow at the sight. He's an accountant he told me earlier. I watch him computing the sum of this wealth. If he offers me only a bowl of noodles for lunch I'll refuse him. It would be an insult after all the time I've spent with them. If he offers me noodles with pork, bits of green onion and egg I might relent. It would still be an insult but not such a grave one.

I save the Pavilion of Ten Thousand Happinesses for last. The eighteen-meter statue of the Maitreya Buddha carved from a single piece of white sandalwood was included in the Guinness Book of Records in 1993. It's a knockout and will undoubtedly insure a five-course lunch with mandarin oranges swimming in a bowl of sugar syrup for dessert.

"My God," the wife whispers. Even the weasel can't conceal his awe. The two of them gasp, their necks bent as if receiving a sacred host.

"Thank you so much." She opens her purse. "We may have missed it without you." I'm hoping she'll extract some extra yuan for my services besides the lunch that I anticipate. But she only removes a tissue to dab at her eyes which have begun to tear with excitement.

"It's a wow all right." The weasel checks his watch. "Better move along, honey. We want to see that Confucius Temple before lunch."

"I can show you that too. It's just across the street. Much quieter there. Not so many tourists. You'll enjoy it." I recall a good restaurant around the corner from the Confucius Temple. It has an excellent Peking duck with orange sauce. Their steamed scallops, large and succulent, are also noteworthy.

"Thanks," the weasel says, "We don't want to take any more of your time. We know you have to get back to your studies. Exams coming up I bet."

"Lots of luck. You've been so kind." His wife touches my arm.

"Oh, it's no trouble," I call as I follow them into the street. "I'd be most grateful if you'd allow me—" The growling in my stomach competes with the traffic noise, a cacophony of hunger. But they've already climbed into a cab whose driver will overcharge by circling the block several times before he drops them at the Confucius Temple. It'll serve them right.

Emily

I HAVE RECEIVED A SCHOLARSHIP for English Independent Study at Shandong University in the far city of Jinan. In 1949 Chairman Mao introduced such scholarships to encourage literacy among our people. My grandmother worshiped Mao. She had his picture on all the walls of our little farmhouse. Even out back she had his photo above the hole in the ground my father dug for our necessity. Occasionally I found fly specks on his cheeks. I brushed them off when I helped Grandmother to the outhouse. She had difficulty walking. Her feet were once bound which was the custom in her youth. And even though Mao declared that women should unbind their feet, Grandmother's toes never healed properly. She waddled about like ducks in our pond, slipping easily on the muck. I heard her cry for help, her shrill voice pleading for me to come. From then on, I did not allow her to go to the outhouse alone.

Grandmother encouraged me to apply for this scholarship even though it meant I could no longer care for her. "To learn English is necessary for the young. For me it does not matter. My brain is weak. But for you, dear Emily, the world is ripe as those persimmons waiting to be peeled."

And so, I went, leaving the farm I loved so well, the greenhouse where we raised plump tomatoes and cucumbers long as my arm, fertilizing with droppings from chickens that fluttered about our yard. I traveled on an overnight sleeper. The benches felt hard as stone, six passengers to a compartment, men and women together. Being the youngest and the most limber, they assigned me the top bunk. As I was wearing a skirt, I did not prefer this. Men on lower bunks took advantage of their position, ogling me when I climbed above them. Embarrassed by this, I did not leave my bunk all night even though I wanted to relieve myself in that dingy toilet at the far end of the train.

In the shrouded morning we pulled into an unlit station. I lay in my bunk until all the men left even though they kept offering to help me climb down. I hoped someone from the University would greet me, but no one came. It was very early; the amenities were not open. A lone attendant in blue uniform straggled about with her bamboo broom, collecting cigarette butts littered on the floor, her mouth covered by a white cotton mask, her hands in plastic gloves. I felt as if an unwashed blanket had smothered me, replacing the pure air I breathed at home. My heart ached for home, the cackling chickens, the touch of my grandmother. Even the scolding voices of my parents would have been welcome.

My clothes and hair were rumpled from a sleepless night. Men snored so loud they even outdid the roaring train. I had never been on a train before. Trains frightened me even though Grandmother assured me there was nothing to be scared of. "Trains in China are safe. They will not fly off the tracks as they do in America." I tried to control my fear. I would not disgrace Grandmother.

I untied the scarf she had given me as a farewell present and secured it around my mouth to ward off infection. Buses waited outside the station with multiple destinations, but none seemed to be going to Shandong, that is to the West Campus. The University had many campuses that specialized in particular areas of study. Finally, a slender boy on a rusty bicycle sensed my confusion and offered to take me there. "It's my business." He strapped my belongings on back. "It's not legal, but legal jobs are hard to come by. I invent my own."

A skilled rider, he weaved between cars and buses, carts filled with carrots, cauliflower, huge purple eggplants and tiny yellow squash. Occasionally he swiped a squash passing it to me to slip in his basket, promising to share the booty if I did not report him. "I will never report you. You are the first friend I have made in Jinan."

He gave me a half smile. I could see that one canine was missing, that he tried to conceal it by never smiling fully. In the countryside, dental care was difficult to come by. One must travel many miles to a clinic. I heard such care would be easier to obtain in the city, but perhaps that was just propaganda to lure peasants to the towns for temporary employment on new construction sites.

"I call myself Michael," he hollered as he caught the tail end of a bus. When the bus came to a stop, the driver descended upon him with curses and threats. But Michael pleaded, "I must get this girl to a clinic. She's very sick."

The driver relented, "Be careful. Police are strict in Jinan. They might impound your bicycle." His passengers began to hoot at the delay, so he stomped aboard and drove on amidst the cheering clang of lunch pails.

"Why do you call yourself Michael?" I coughed over the fumes of the departing bus.

"Michael Jackson's cool," he pushed his bike from the curb. "Even when he's hot he's still cool. I want to be like him."

"I heard he used the whitening potion they sell in the market."

"I've tried that stuff. It doesn't work for me, but that's all right. I'm cool in spirit."

I wish I could be cool, I thought, when we hit a puddle left over from the recent rains. It spattered my flip-flops and dirtied my toes. I resembled a migrant worker from my village rather than a student. I felt grateful Grandmother had hidden my new white running shoes inside my clothes roll rather than letting me wear them as I had wished. "You must look smart on campus," she said. "Dirty shoes will make you look stupid."

The buildings were huge in Jinan, almost touching the sky. Some leaned to the side. I feared they would fall upon us. Workers teetered on ladders, pounding and drilling until my ears ached. "Does this go on all day?"

"It never stops. Even by torchlight it continues."

"How do you stand it?"

"You must try to get used to it, even to love it. It's a sign of prosperity. Soon we'll be number one."

"My grandmother says the same. She says that time is coming."

"Just read the news, watch the TV. China's on the rise."

"We do not have the television on my farm."

"Then how did your grandmother know all this?"

"My father talks to the tradesmen when he sells our vegetables in the city. He brings back old newspapers. I read them to my grandmother. Her eyes do not work well, but she still knows many things."

"We're here." He swerved the bike to avoid the guards waiting at the University gate. They were busy directing traffic in and out of the sprawling campus. On an adjacent field students played soccer and volleyball amidst cheers from fans crowding walkways. I could hardly wait to be part of that excitement.

"Wait here." The guard held Michael's handlebars. He could not pass.

"She's a new student," he said. "I'm taking her to her dorm."

"Which dorm you in, Miss?" He peered down at my feet with suspicion.

"I am a scholarship student." I dragged my certificate from my satchel where it lay buried beneath the books I brought from home: an edition of Shakespeare's plays in Chinese, several novels by the Bronte sisters, particularly Emily, my favorite, and the Nancy Drew mysteries I had read as a child. Simple English helped me to master the language.

"Scholarship students are across street, behind clinic." He inspected my certificate and waved it back to me, unimpressed.

"Behind the clinic? Why am I not on this campus with the other students?"

"University regulations. Scholarship students not regular students."

"What do you mean?'

"They separate group. If you scholarship student you never be University student."

"I do not believe that."

"You find out."

Michael careened into honking cars.

"Careful." I grabbed the handlebars. An auto screeched its brakes.

"They never wait." Michael rang his bell. "You have to be a tiger."

Feeling a twinge inside, I hugged the crossbar, knees shaking. We cycled into the clinic's courtyard. Freshmen students in khaki uniforms paraded like real soldiers. How I would love to be one of them. How I would cherish such a uniform even if it meant I must march every day. I would be a true student then, able to afford my tuition, not a hanger-on, a scholarship student from the farm, too poor to afford the University. Being poor in new China seemed a disgrace.

Michael unstrapped my roll and helped me tie it on my back. "I'll carry your books for you." He reached for my satchel.

"I can do it."

"It would please me, Emily." He locked his bike among other bikes, paint peeling, tires threadbare.

"How did you know my name?"

"I guessed. All that Emily Bronte in your satchel. It was either Emily or Nancy. I knew it couldn't be Shakespeare."

"You are right. I will never be that smart."

"I like that name, Emily. It's cool.

"As cool as Michael?"

"Almost."

He danced to the back of the clinic while the freshmen applauded. I followed him to a dirty courtyard strewn with broken cement, lunch wrappers and beer cans. In the midst of debris stood an isolated building. Air conditioners fronted the windows, increasing the cacophony of the clinic. Clotheslines with girls' panties and pajamas clung to the sides of the collapsing structure.

When we reached the door, he handed me my books. "Good luck in your studies. And don't pay any attention to that gate guard. I don't think he knows what he's talking about."

"Thank you." I pulled some yuan from my satchel, but he hurried off.

Suddenly he turned, "Maybe I'll see you around."

"Maybe…" A thread of hope filled me. I remembered Grandmother sewing the very dress I wore. I would not let her down.

Heavy rain began to pelt me. I rushed inside to protect my books. Moisture would surely destroy their tattered pages. I had purchased them at a bookstall during one of my infrequent trips to the city with my father where, after a good harvest, I would help him sell vegetables. Returning late, I read by flashlight. Our electricity was sometimes out after a storm, but more often my father chose to cut the power. He was saving money against the next harvest which might fail. He needed to put something aside.

I had not relieved myself for some hours. In desperation, I searched for the nearest toilet. Finally, in an alcove, I saw the sign, WC. The stench was almost unbearable, but there was no alternative. I squatted above the hole, my feet straddling the sides.

I wanted to clean myself, but there was no water or paper in the cubicle or in the sink outside, a common hand washing area for men and women. Only an old rag hung on a hook, a reminder that at one time the faucet worked.

The hallway was lined with rooms bearing numbers. Boys were on the first two floors, girls on the third and fourth. On the main campus they had separate buildings. Boys waved, strummed guitars, calling to me as I passed. I hurried to the third floor searching the corridor for room 313.

In the center of the corridor, a large kitchen held a huge water filter and some burners for cooking. Mops and brooms leaned in a corner beside plastic garbage sacks. Empty coke cans escaped an opening. A few peels of onion and garlic littered the counters amidst grains of rice and scraps of steamed bread. My stomach grumbled. I hadn't eaten since yesterday. As I reached for a bite of bread, I heard a voice behind me and turned. A chubby girl stood there with hair black as mine and glasses so thick I hardly saw her eyes. She held out her hand, "You must be Emily. They told me you would be our sixth roommate."

"You are Willow, the one who wrote to me?"

"Don't laugh. My parents hoped I'd grow willowy as Jinan's special tree. It never happened."

She flung my roll over her shoulder. "Our room's beside the staircase. It's noisy. Metal doors make a big bang at night. But you get used to it."

She opened our room. Six bunks adorned the gray walls, one on top of the other. "Since you're last to arrive, you get the top bunk next to an air conditioner.

You can use your clothes as a pillow. No closet, only those hooks on the wall."

The room seemed to swell. I thought I must be getting a head cold. I longed for our farm, the cerulean sky afloat with clouds so dense they could be snow cones at the fair.

"Bathroom's down the hall. We take turns for showers. Hot water's only a brief period morning and night." She inspected my toes.

My stomach growled so loud it embarrassed me, but I could not control it.

"You must be hungry. Come, I'll take you to the cafeteria. It's on the main campus. Lunch is almost over, but there should be something left."

She locked our door. "You have to be careful. Theft is rampant."

We clomped our way down an echoing staircase. There was no way one could sneak out of here. We crossed the courtyard. Students played volleyball amidst rubbish. Then we were into traffic. Willow grabbed my hand, dragging me between honking autos and colliding bicycles. "You have to be a tiger," she chanted. We jostled our way onto the campus.

A thick yellow pall hung over the University. It seemed difficult to discriminate between statues and people. Ghostlike buildings hovered between bare trees. Nearing the cafeteria, bright banners emerged from the pall, flying like signals from another world. Students mobbed tables to sign up for fall activities.

"Have you signed?" I asked Willow. She did not answer, so I repeated my question.

"Scholarship students can't join in campus activities, but you get used to it." Her glasses fogged. I had the feeling Willow would never get used to it and neither would I.

"Cafeteria's on four levels." She pushed aside the plastic streamers that deterred insects from entering. "The most expensive food's at top. We'll eat on first level."

The only items left were rice and steamed bread with a few dishes of pickled cabbage. "It's a limited menu down here, but it's cheap. You don't have your food card yet so I'll treat."

"I wish to repay you." I offered some yuan.

Willow pushed them away. "It's my pleasure today. Tomorrow it'll be yours."

We laughed carrying steamed bread to a table only partially cleared. Chicken bones mixed with slops of vegetable soup and tea. It was late. Workers were eating lunch, paying no attention to debris. "Is it always this messy?"

"You get used to it." Willow flipped a chicken bone to the floor.

Pulling apart the huge white glob of steamed bread, I stuffed it in my mouth the way Willow did. At this time of day at home we would be sitting together for our midday lunch of fresh tomatoes and cucumbers, steamed squash and baby carrots with big bowls of fried rice topped with bits of egg and chicken. How I longed for my mother's cooking.

"Would you like to visit the student market?" she asked while we chewed the last bits of bread.

We left the cafeteria to workers, who shouted to each other above clattering pots and pans.

The student market was cramped, shelves bursting with everything from Adidas to apples. "I'll leave you here." Willow dropped some oranges into her basket. The clerk weighed them, carefully placing the fruit in a plastic sack and marking the price. Willow waved on her way to the cash register. "I must attend English corner. Can you find your way back?"

"No problem." My stomach churned at the thought of crossing traffic without Willow.

"Well then, I'll let you explore but don't be late. Your roommates are cooking dinner tonight. Tomorrow it'll be our turn."

A sense of panic engulfed me among the rows of Lay's potato chips, Hershey bars and Snyder's pretzels. Most items were imported from America. Suddenly, I heard a clear American voice on the other side of the aisle. How I wished to speak American like the actors I had seen on television when my father took me to the city.

I peeked between boxes of Quaker Oats and Cheerios, Rice Cakes and Fruit Loops. "May I join you?" I whispered, afraid the tall blonde teacher would say no. She already had a circle of students trying to imitate her accent.

"Of course," she smiled pushing a strand of hair behind a dangling earring. I rushed to the other side of the aisle before she changed her mind.

"What dorm are you in?" She fingered a pretty lavender package of sour plums.

I thought of lying, of pretending I was a regular student for fear she might dismiss me if she knew the truth. But I must learn to be a tiger. I breathed in hard, then heard myself say, "I live in the Scholarship Dorm, behind the clinic."

"Oh," she opened the package, her fingernails long and delicate, pink as the lotus on our lake. Someday I will have nails like that, I thought.

"You must be very smart to have a scholarship," she said. And seeing the other students turn their backs to me, she offered me a plum.

Bago Station

THERE IS NO PLACE for me but Bago, once one of the most important cities in Burma, now a forgotten stop on Myanmar's line to Mandalay. I wait each day at Bago Station. There are trains arriving from Yangon every morning and early afternoon. Occasionally, instead of the bus, tourists ride the open-air train with the workers. It is cheap, only US one dollar, instead of the bus, two people three hundred kyat, or the taxi, forty to fifty dollars US. They arrive full of train dust, determined to view our great Buddhas and holy altars, to inhale the incense, the cumin and coriander, to lose themselves in the rumble of trucks traveling Bago night and day, making sleep almost impossible.

This morning two persons arrived, a man much older than myself, (for I am thirty but look thirteen. It is the rice that does it, a single bowl each morning, like the monks in our monastery on the hill) and with him an old woman. The man, very white and somewhat weak looking, helped the old woman from the train as if she were parchment and could crack if she did not step carefully. The train steps are steep. Sometimes they are missing altogether, and the passengers must leap from the train throwing their baggage before them.

The train from Yangon to Bago was late this morning. Engine trouble they said. This is not unusual. The train from Yangon is often late. I wait and wait until dark. Sometimes it does not arrive at all and I am left to bicycle home in the blackness. This is treacherous as the roads are rough; pot holes the size of graves waiting to catch you. I have fallen into several of these, bruising arms and legs, wrecking my bike which fortunately my friend Tan could repair. My second wife bathed my bruises while our baby sloshed in the bath water. "Get another job," she scolded. "This one is too dangerous."

"What other job? There is no job but Bago Station." She knows this as well as I. Tourists are our only income unless we become rice farmers, burning the fields before new planting, our faces black with soot. I tried that when I was younger. She did not like that either. The soot was difficult to wash. I remained black until burning season was over.

My two tourists seem confused. Tourists always look confused. There are no signs telling them which way the great Buddhas lie, or the Ruff & Ready hotel, or a toilet to relieve themselves.

I approach smiling my best smile. "Let me help you. I have lived here all my life."

"Where is the ticket window?" the man asks wiping the dust from his oversized sun glasses. "We need to book a train back to Yangon this evening."

I lead them to the ticket office. It is a cubicle hidden near the back of the train station. The clerk is nowhere in sight. "He must be at lunch. Sit, he will soon be here." But of course, there is no place to sit so they stand leaning against the doorjamb to rest. Finally, he comes, sipping tea from a thermos.

"Passports?" He swallows slowly, seating himself behind his cluttered desk.

My tourist unfolds them from a money belt hidden beneath his shirt. "Train to Yangon tonight?"

"All booked," the clerk answers, rubbing his belly which overlaps his belt. "There might be a bus."

"Where is the bus depot?" The old lady looks flustered as if this could not be happening.

"That way." He points outside."

"Do you have a map?"

The clerk smiles, waving his hand, and chattering in Burmese, addresses the next person in line. My tourists start to walk, probably thinking they can walk everywhere in Bago. They have no idea of the breadth of this city, how the Buddhas are at opposite ends. It would take a week or more to walk to them all.

"Come." I take my advantage. "I will guide you to the bus depot."

The bus depot is almost impossible to find as it is not really a depot but part of a coffee shop. Feng runs it. She has the schedule. She knows when the last bus to Yangon will arrive. "Five p.m.," she says. "Be here. The bus will not wait."

It is now two p.m. in the afternoon. My tourists are gray with train dust and tired. "Come, I will show you the Buddhas."

They hesitate. "Can we walk there?"

"It is too far. I have a friend who will take us. Four passenger bus, very comfortable."

"What is the price?" The man fumbles beneath his shirt.

I knew he would ask that. They always do. It is often the first thing from their mouths. They are afraid we will cheat them. But that is not my custom. I want only what is fair. "Twenty-five kyat." I bargain.

"Twenty," he says.

"Twenty-five," I repeat thinking if I say it often enough he'll give in.

"Twenty-two," he answers firmly.

I agree, tired of repeating myself but also because I notice two other guides waiting to steal my tourists from me.

My friend Tan waits with his Tuk-tuk parked in back of the cafe. "This is Tan. He will drive us to all the Buddhas."

"We must be back by five." The old lady looks a bit jittery.

"You will be. I promise."

I help them into the Tuk-tuk. It is not easy as the steps are loose and the seat boards rickety. The old lady

hits her head on the metal rods upholding the cardboard roof.

"I thought you had a van." She rubs the sore spot
on her head.

"This is a van," I shout as Tan revs his motor bike.

The Tuk-tuk rocks forward shooting the old woman
across the aisle. Her son catches her.

"We could use some seat belts," she mumbles.

"Yes, I have ordered some from Amazon. They will
arrive any day now." I laugh knowing this is impossible.
There is no such service in Bago. Very few have com-
puters. I am hoping to buy one second hand from one
of the monks at the monastery on the hill. The monks
have all the money exacting a price for their prayers. I
am sending my older son to the monastery as I can no
longer afford to send him to school. He will learn to be
a monk, to beg for donations, to chant prayers at certain
hours, to obey orders. This last will be difficult for him as
he runs from me whenever I catch him stealing mangoes
from our neighbor's garden. Our neighbor sells them
in town so it is not right that my son should steal them.

Tan steers through the vendors selling fruit and
fish, chicken and beef, all the foodstuffs that I cannot
afford. Flies settle on the chicken, making a home on
the gizzards. The smell of overripe bananas overcomes
the old lady. She presses a tissue to her nose as if to
ward off some disease. I love the perfume of overripe
fruit. It is a reminder of plenty. Fruit could not get overripe if there were none.

We approach the Shemawdaw Pagoda. It is often referred to as the Golden God Temple. It is the tallest pagoda in Myanmar. I help my old lady from the Tuk-tuk. She stumbles gawking at the Golden God.

"Steady." I take her elbow.

A government official approaches. "Ten-dollar entrance." He holds up *Lonely Planet* to prove the entrance fee.

My tourists look surprised. Obviously, they have never read this travel guide to Southeast Asia. "Come." Hurriedly we reboard the Tuk-tuk. I take them to the secondary entrance. "No fee here. Avoid passing the western gate."

The old lady does not wish to take her shoes off. Perhaps her toes are crooked and she does not wish to show them.

"Mom," her son says, "we have to take our shoes off. It is disrespectful not to."

"I'm not taking them off. That's final." She starts to climb aboard the Tuk-tuk. Tan rushes to help her. She smiles at him. He holds her hand longer than is necessary. It is Tan's way. He drives quickly to the other pagodas as time is growing short.

The Shwethalyaung Reclining Buddha is my favorite. It is the second largest Buddha in the world. I could lie beside this Buddha all night. Secretly I have done this, sneaking in after dark, spending the whole night pressed against its feet, kissing them, praying for my first wife's happiness in the next life. Praying the dengue fever did not accompany her into the world she inhabits now. Praying she is relieved from all sickness, her beauty returned to her, the beauty she lost during the long fever. They could not attend to her at the hospital as I had no kyat to pay for her care. She was placed on a cot in the corridor and left to die there.

"It is four p.m. now," I remind Tan. We have seen the Kyaik Pun Pagoda as well and the Maha Kalyani Sima, and the Mahazedi Pagoda, the Shwegugale Pagoda and finally the Snake Pagoda which my tourists loved as the entrance was free. "A bit like Disneyland," the old lady blurts, her eyes glazed with pagodas.

I have seen this Disneyland on Feng's TV when I wait for the bus to Yangon. It is true that our colors are bright like Mickey Mouse, the Seven Dwarfs, and Alice in her Wonderland. We take great care of our Buddhas, repainting them often, gilding the stupas, making certain the altars are swept clean. If we are careful of our holy sites in this world, we are promised a better life in the next.

Tan starts his motor. It catches, then stops. I help him give the bike a shove. "Get on." I yell. "Once it gets going we can't stop. "

But the old lady won't get on. "Get a taxi. I'm not getting on that thing. I value my life."

"You must get on," Tan pleads. "It is the only way. No taxis out here."

"C'mon, Mom," her son urges. "We'll miss the bus."

"I don't want to die in that contraption," she sobs.

Finally, we carry her on, seating her between us, holding her steady as Tan rocks the motor bike trying to get it started. Ru—n-ru—n-ru—n— He sweats. Crowds gather, some laughing, some trying to help push the Tuk-tuk over the ruts.

"They promised us a new road," Tan calls back. "It is late in coming. Maybe never."

We jolt forward and gradually begin to fly over the ruts as the crowd waves us on. Tan hoots as we speed toward the bus stop. Even the old lady has stopped complaining.

"The bus for Yangon left five minutes ago. It wouldn't wait." Feng sloshes some coffee cups in a pail of water. "Take them to the Ruff & Redy. Ask for a room in back. The old lady needs some sleep."

www.ingramcontent.com/pod-product-compliance
Lightning Source LLC
Chambersburg PA
CBHW020655260626
47157CB00008B/3039